I HAVE NOT ANSWERED

Adam Grydehøj

I Have Not Answered

Beewolf

BEEWOLF PRESS

Published in Denmark
by Beewolf Press
an imprint of Island Dynamics
Blågårds Plads 1, st., 2200 Copenhagen N
http://www.beewolfpress.com

Copyright © Adam Grydehøj 2014

ISBN: 978-87-996331-0-4

All rights reserved. No part of this publication may be reproduced, stored in a retrieval system, or transmitted in any form or by any means, electronic, mechanical, photocopying, recording, or otherwise, without the prior permission of the publisher.

Cover photograph, 'March Day', © David Gifford.

Thus, I had so long suffered in this quest,
Heard failure prophesied so oft, been writ
So many times among 'The Band' – to wit,
The knights who to the Dark Tower's search addressed
Their steps – that just to fail as they, seemed best,
And all the doubt was now – should I be fit?

Robert Browning
'Childe Roland to the Dark Tower Came'

Prologue

I woke as from a dream, the past spread out before me.

A girl looked up at me, her head in my lap. I stroked her long black hair, and my skin paled against it. Then she turned her blue eyes toward the sea, encroached all around by close dark sky. These blue eyes, they were filled with sorrow and with love, as if the one emotion occasioned the other but with such intimate causality that it was impossible to discern which had come first.

Before us stood a harp.

Its strings vibrated still.

Once a thing has been moved, it can never again attain a state of rest. A residue of movement remains, a residual shuddering through the epochs and dwindling down in time until all visible signs have been effaced.

But the memory of movement is still.

A whole procession of consequences and causes stretches back and forth, like the string of a harp. Or perhaps the rim of a chalice, circling endlessly as you trace it with your fingertip. The circle is closed: I cannot say where my story ends and the next one begins.

But *this*, surely, was my story, my sacrifice and no one else's. All that I had lived when awake was to prepare me for this dream. Or had all my dreaming prepared me for this life? At that moment, the time – which has been so long – belonged to me.

But what came next, I do not know, for on the horizon an island was calling, dead and black. Whether the island was itself hateful or whether its hate was a reflection of us on the opposite shore, I cannot say.

Yet it was calling.

And when I answered this call, I woke as from a dream. The girl's face was gone and my memory lapsed, all in bits.

But my word is still.

The new day was clear, with scuttles of cloud far to the southeast. Before me lay an island, calling out across the waters.

Part I

I KNOW A PLACE where there are lights in the hill at night. At times, I have even seen them myself.

It has happened, perhaps, on two or three occasions. I know the lights are there, so it does not matter whether I see them. From the moment I first saw them, I knew they were there, and they will remain there until they one day cease to be. When that day comes, I am quite certain I will never know it, for one cannot, surely, know of a thing that does not exist.

At the windward base of the head of Murnin Kame sits a cottage. Other houses are in the lee of the headland, but whether they are thus more favoured, I cannot say, for there is a certain dampness there, where the waters settle, having seeped down from the meeting of the ridges that form the firth.

But this little cottage. It is painted white, flaking, with grey stone showing beneath. There are windows along the lengths and one in the narrowness at the west end, behind the threadbare yellow armchair, with a pink ceramic lamp on a little table beside. I understand the website calls it a *reading table*. Though I have never bothered to check, so it might just be a thing that is said. The yellow threadbare armchair was brought up on the North Boat from Aberdeen and was reupholstered once. But that was before the oil and the roads and the leisure centres. And the IKEA in Aberdeen, which perhaps does not even sell yellow armchairs. For all I know.

The window behind the armchair overlooks a field ending in sky, where land drops into sea. From out the north window, the land descends more gradually, and a wedge of ocean is visible, though not yet the beach, which is curved out of sight.

To the right of this window is the door outside, and in front of the window is another table, larger than the first. People use this table for various things. Some put their suitcases on it when unpacking, but it is also a convenient place to take one's meal. *Roughing it*, they say.

There is a laptop computer on the table at the moment. Across the room from the table is a bed, which is used for sleeping. They also read on it sometimes, but I have never heard it called a *reading bed*. The window behind the bed overlooks the hillside, too far down the ridge to see the lights. At the east end of this room is a doorway leading to a little kitchen with a new mini-fridge, an old gas cooker, and access to the toilet and shower. It is basic, but they say that is why people come here.

Out the door of the cottage, a flagged path leads to an excellent blacktop road. Two hundred yards down the road to the east is a modern house, considerably larger than the cottage and built in two levels.

Outside the door to this house stands a young man from South. He reminds me of something. I know there is a thing I should be thinking, but all I remember is that I should be thinking it. He is clean-shaven, and though he is not fat, he is somewhat soft around the middle. His life is without meaning, yet his mind is too little refined to comprehend this fact.

He is like all the others.

He should be frowning, for he is hungry, and the morning is late. But this young man is very well trained. He really does smile nicely.

★

THE DOOR OPENED.

"Good morning," the young man said.

Margaret saw his smile, and she smiled too. "Oh, yes. And how are you finding it?"

"Lovely. Quite a view."

"Won't you...?" she gestured inside.

The young man took off his boots though they were not muddy. "I didn't know about the shop."

"You mean—?"

"I didn't want to cause him any trouble. He said he'd have some bread in this afternoon, and he offered to sell me some tins. But of course, I haven't an opener."

"We're just hardly a village. The shop only stocks on order."

"I understand."

"You can buy most things in Walls. You won't find a real shop before Lerwick. But you're on bike of course. I never thought."

He followed her to the kitchen. Last week's *Shetland Times* was on the table, opened to the vacancies section.

"It's silly, you know." Margaret shook her head. The gesture could have meant any number of things. "I should've thought. Everyone comes by car. You're the first in, oh, fifteen-odd years."

"It gives me a feel for the landscape. See things as people saw them before cars."

Margaret opened a tin of beans. "It was by water then. There weren't roads for biking, I tell you that." She laid two strips of bacon sizzling on the pan. "It's only after the oil."

He pointed to the food on the stovetop. "Is that—?" He feigned surprise. "That's not for me, is it? Oh, no. Really. I didn't mean—"

"Now, now," said Margaret. "Now, now. You're our guest, aren't you? Can't have you starving." Two eggs joined the bacon. "But I'm not from these parts, you know."

"Oh?"

"No." She laughed. "I'm from town. My mother was Scottish."

"A herring girl?"

"You do know our history. She was a herring girl indeed."

★

I Have Not Answered

But let me tell you about Shetland.

In winter, it can be very dark, especially away from town, without all the streetlights.

Then in summer, it can be light all day and night so you nearly cannot see. That is a strange thing about the night-time summer light, when the sun seems to filter through a great pane of frosted glass brought up on the North Boat. High in the sky, beyond our reach, the sun's stream is separated and distinguished, and the light rains down on the land all in bits, with glimpses of darkness in between. In those glimpses, if you strain hard enough, you can hear echoes of the time of those who came before.

This light, it is called the *simmer dim*. And when it is cloudy, the clouds part here and there, and that disparate light pours through the holes in torrents. Splotches of sea light up as by a flash of herring, and the land glows an obscene gold-grey, like something from that artist fellow Turner.

A guest once left behind a book about him. It was mainly pictures. Paintings of trees and buildings and things. I recognised none of the places. But the light was that of Shetland.

While the young man was taking his breakfast, I went back to the cottage and looked through his papers on the big table. I do not normally read their papers, but the young man had been up writing so late the night before as to arouse my curiosity. The guests are no business of mine, and I do not bother about them in the least. But they serve to pass the time.

Which is, after all, so long.

Dear Sal, he had written. *I want you to know I've arrived and everything's fine. It's a lovely old place here, really far out in the country, like grandmother's. The kitchen and bathroom are small but OK. There's a big writing table in the living room and an ancient yellow chair. The owner is one of those kind doting types. Anyway I'll start work tomorrow and will go around and say hello to people.*

How did your exam go? Sorry I didn't call but it just felt weird using the mobile in a place like this. Anyway I'll get over it!! I'll call tomorrow. Promise.

And listen: Don't worry. We'll work things out. It could happen to anyone, right? They say it makes relationships stronger.

Love, Innes.

And that was almost all he wrote. But he had an afterthought just before going to bed, and he wrote at the bottom, *I'm thinking of you tonight.*

It is funny how they write these things that will not be read for days. By the time she gets the letter and knows he is thinking of her, he will be thinking of something else. I have heard *it is something about ink on paper*, but I have also heard *it is something about the handwritten word* and am not at all certain these mean the same thing. But it does seem to affect them. Some do not even bring their phones on the trip. Or they take out the batteries and put them in their suitcases, like some kind of ritual.

This one did not take the battery out of his phone. But he did something else that was very queer. Almost as soon as he had come in, before he had started writing to Sal even, he took from his suitcase a purple silken pouch, its neck closed up with string. From this pouch, he removed a stone and a ceramic plate and set them on the reading table. The stone was a deep green. It is a type of stone called *jade*. I know this, for I once saw such stones in the shop in town that sold crystals and shiny things.

And here is what is strange: This stone was carved in the shape of a little sitting man who wore on his head a cap of beads. His hands met at the knuckles upon crossed legs, with the soles of his feet facing up. And his squinty little eyes were closed as if in sleep.

The ceramic plate was white and shaped like a flower, with petals all around. At first I thought these were trinkets acquired at the airport gift shop. Now I would not hazard to guess, for the young man proceeded to place an odd little rough brown cone in the very centre of the plate and attempted to light the top of it with a match. But the fire would not keep, and instead, the tip of the cone just glowed orange, emitting a strange odour that swirled up in smoke.

The smell had lingered in the room most of the night, causing my head to ache and driving me back out onto the hill, where the air was fresh with salt.

But now it was different, for when the young man returned from breakfast, he smelled of beans, eggs, bacon, and toast. He sat down at the big table — *the writing table* — directly after coming in and picked up a pen. I thought he would write to Sal again, but he instead took out a notebook and wrote on the cover page, *Fieldnotes. Shetland. Innes Pitmedden.* It looked very impressive, very official.

When he turned to the next page, he wrote in a tiny, meticulous hand, different from the looser print in the letter to Sal. *10 July. Spoke with Margaret Stevens at breakfast. Did not see Graham Stevens. A daughter May is in Glasgow. Someone in family looking for work. I have said I am interested in stories but have not mentioned the particular story. When Shuldham-Shaw collected songs in the 1950s, he was told that a West Mainland man named Paul Stevens knew a story like 'King Orfeo'. The Shetland 'King Orfeo' ballad has a happy ending, like the Middle English 'Sir Orfeo' poem, derived from Old French. Scandinavian Orpheus-type ballads can have either happy or sad endings. If the Shetland prose tale ends sadly, it could prove a second route of migration into Scotland for the Orpheus legend. That could revolutionise scholarship on Child Ballad 19, not to mention 39 and 41.*

The young man put down his pen and smiled, this time for his own sake rather than for anyone else.

★

I WAS ROOTING AROUND in the peat atop Murnin Kame, looking for living things. They are not, then they are, then they are dead. Yet in that short space when they are, they hold a bit of interest. These little soulless things usually suffice. But this day, they did not. There is so much time in which to do things yet so few things to do.

I Have Not Answered

And so I thought that maybe I should go see what the young man was doing. I am unsure what it is he does, but he certainly does a lot of it.

I picked up his trail from the door of the cottage and followed it to Netherdale, where the young man was standing beside the phone booth. A gull rose out of Voe of Dale and swept low over his head, then north toward Ramna Vord. The young man swung around and watched the bird until it was out of sight. He kept staring after it for a time, seeking that obscure point at which all things disappear.

Leaving the road, he followed Burn of Dale down to the sea, where the stream dispersed in the shingle on the beach. The day was clear, but it was just past noon, so the summer light was not yet strange. Foula squatted out in the Atlantic, a great hunk of rock with a thin veneer of green. The young man glanced at the island. Taking out his notebook, he wrote, *Foula. 20 miles west of Walls. Ferry connections to Walls/Scalloway. Settled by Vikings in 9th Century. Now owned by Holbourn family. Population under 30. Sandstone, variety of subarctic flora.*

It appeared as if the island were beckoning him. But in fact, it looks at everyone that way. From certain angles, Foula appears so kind and gentle, yet if you come at it from the west, down by the foot of the Kame, it is all cliffs and horror, a wall of hateful rock uprising past the sky. Souls have been lost there, I assure you, in the dark gap between water and stone. Beyond the elemental passions, there is simply nothing. And that is the worst place to be.

From the beach at Voe of Dale, however, you might imagine Foula wished you well.

The young man took out his Ordnance Survey map and rolled the place names around his mouth. "Clett. Buid Stacks. The Groud. The Rigg. Runkie Head," and so on up the coast. These visitors deceive themselves in thinking the language palpable, somehow more real than their own tongue.

But this young man, he is not so entirely predictable. I have seen him in the cottage, working on a queer thing. It is a big sheet of tough paper that needs to be folded to fit on the writing table. He has drawn on it a map of the west of the Westside, referring to the Ordnance Survey map for all the particulars. But here is what is queer: He has written on his map the names of all sorts of people who live places, and he has drawn lines between some of them with a ruler. The Stevens, the Nevins, the Millars, the Neelys, the Spences, the Smiths, and all the rest, each at their own separate houses, represented by little black boxes joined up with lines, wonderful straight. Lines are not that straight in real life. But anyway. All these people in their little clusters, with lines going out between.

I was thinking this as he inspected the remains of the noosts on the beach, to which the boats were drawn in the old days. Back then, in the haaf fishing, before the time of any of them yet living, the quantity of whitefish landed here—you would not believe it. The men at the splitting boards would set to work, then the fish was salted and left to dry. Back then, I had food in abundance. The food was not varied, but it was abundant.

I Have Not Answered

Before I knew it, the young man was off the beach and up the slope north of the voe. By the time I caught up, he had reached the point of the ness. He looked north past the headland and let his eyes rest on the low hills of Papa, serene across the sound. Then he glanced back at distant Foula. I suppose he was comparing the two islands, but they are not at all alike.

The young man worked his way along the coast—around Coppa Wick, above the sheerness of Sel Ayre, and down into Deepdale. I left him there to continue his journey alone.

I never go into Deepdale if I can help it. And I knew he would be back, for he had but a small bag with him.

So I waited there, sometimes on the cliffs, just throwing pebbles down at Erne's Stack, trying to hit the sharpness of it.

And sometimes across Blouk Field, peering into Deepdale. If you look carefully, you can sometimes see them moving down there, on both sides of the burn. They would like to cross over to the other side, but they cannot when the burn is flowing. And when the burn freezes and is covered with snow, they all cross over to one another's side and like it just as little.

It was late before the young man returned. I first noticed him when he was far out along the ridge of Ramna Vord. He had been coming along, I suppose, in plain sight all the way from Sandness Hill, but I had been inattentive. He was about to begin the descent into Deepdale when he paused and looked out to the southwest.

He gazed toward Foula. The light then was just as I told you before, all in bits. And there was Foula, floating like the hull of some upturned ship with drowning men beneath. But the young man could not see it as I could. I imagined what it looked like to him. A great whale singing in the half-light perhaps.

For a moment, I even thought I too could glimpse this beauty. But I knew it was an illusion, so the beauty quickly passed. I could see through the gaps in the mist of light and knew the darkness that lay between.

★

THE YOUNG MAN left the road, turning onto the track that led to Gaet House. The track had formerly continued to Hulter Loch, but after the Council had laid water pipes, it had fallen into disuse and was soon devoured by the grasses.

The Millars have stayed at Gaet House since long ago, but as it is just a little croft house, scarcely reformed, I should think John Millar will be the last to live there.

As the young man walked up the track, he sensed he was being watched, for he hesitated slightly in mid-step, then proceeded as before. A subtle scan of the house located the watcher, a face observing his progress from a window. The young man did not let on but kept walking. A muddy patch spread across the path close by the house. Instead of skirting it, he tramped through the middle. He came in without knocking.

"Hello, John," he called out, removing his boots.

Around the corner, a voice said, "Don't bother with your boots, boy. Carpet's had worse than that."

The young man entered the room and sat next to John. "My son Laurie."

Laurie was in the armchair beside the window. Even sitting, he looked tall and powerful, very practical. His clothes were a bit ragged, and his hands were rough.

"Laurie works with computers," John said. "For the Council." He rose and left the room.

The young man took out his equipment and started arranging it on the sofa table. From the kitchen came the clink of mugs and the rush of the kettle being filled.

Laurie eyed the digital audio recorder. "Dat's an aafil braa machine, is dat."

"From the university. Stereo and ten hours' recording. Bi-directional microphone." The young man adjusted the microphone on its tripod.

John came in with the tray of coffee and biscuits and set it down beside the recorder. "Now, Laurie, you're not speaking Shetland to the man, surely? He'll not understand it."

"It's fine," the young man said. "I'm glad to hear some dialect. It's not so different from the Doric around Aberdeen."

Laurie frowned. He said to his father, "If we dunna spaek Shetlaend i wir ain hame, we canna ax dat fock frae Sooth respeck it." Turning to the young man, he said, "What my father does is called *knappin*. It's when you try saying your thoughts in English. But English is a foreign language, heavy on the tongue. There are dialect words you can't translate."

The young man clicked on the recorder.

"Innes here is studying Shetland," John said. "It's him staying with Margaret. Wants to learn all about Shetland folk."

"First thing," said Laurie, "is we're not Scottish, and we're not Norwegian. We're our own folk."

The young man took a biscuit, holding a hand under his chin to catch crumbs. "Actually, I'd like to hear about trows."

Laurie laughed. "Trows?"

"Stories about trows."

John nodded. "He's been having me recollect the old tales. He calls trows *fairies*."

The young man said, "Different places have different names for the same thing. In Scotland, they're *fairies*. In Denmark, they're *elverfolk*. In Norway, they're *huldre* or *trolls*. In Japan, they're *yokai*. And in Shetland, they're *trows*."

"Those are just stories," said Laurie. "You'll be here a long while if you're looking for trows in the hills."

"He knows they're just tales, boy," John said.

Laurie said, "It's Graham you should speak with. He's the one knows the old stories and that."

"Graham Stevens? Margaret's husband?"

"Aye. His father was one for tales, wasn't he, Daa?"

"He was. Paul Stevens."

Laurie said, "I remember him telling about trows when I was a bairn. After all, they're hardly stories for grown men."

"Paul's been dead these twenty years," said John.

The young man asked Laurie, "Could you tell me any of his stories yourself?"

"No, man. Those are Paul's tales."

John nodded. "I've been saying. Paul had his own way."

Laurie said, "You won't find many folk who'd tell Paul's tales. Except maybe Graham."

"You know," said the young man, "I've not actually seen Graham. Which is strange since I stay just down the road."

John and Laurie glanced at one another. They thought the young man would not notice, but he is practiced in these things.

"Yun Stevens lass has come home from South for the summer," Laurie said. "I've been meaning to go welcome her back. I'll maybe have a word about you speaking with her father. It'll do the man no harm to talk with one like yourself."

John glanced at his son again and then looked down at the audio recorder. "Well. It's a tale you've come for? I'm no great storyteller, Innes, as you're aware."

"You're brilliant, John, really."

"Flattery," said Laurie. "You'll be a true Shetlander yet."

"Well," said John, easing into a heavier accent. "Well. About the trows. You've maybe heard of the trows sometimes taking a liking to folk. Like them so much, they want to keep them. This story's of that sort.

"See, there's a man called Jones living up on Yell. Aye, Jones isn't a Shetland name. Where his folk came frae, I couldna say. But that's what he's called. And he was a braaly good fiddler. Not a prodigy. There was better than him on Yell at the time. But he was good enough to play dances and that. Gave him some income on the side, ken?"

"Whereabouts?" asked Laurie.

"Up by Mid-Yell. I dunna ken precisely where. But he played all over the island. And there's this one winter's night he's engaged to play at a wedding party up in Colvister. So Jones sets out frae the house with his fiddle and has a bit of a walk ahead of him. It's been snowing all week, and he's having no small trouble getting through it. It's not like the Council was running snowploughs up and down Yell those days. As the hours is passing, he gets a bit worried right enough that he'll not make it to the party on time. And then the wind picks up and is blowing the snow well nigh horizontal, and our man here, he canna hardly see a thing as he's trudging along. He just follows the path best he can. But what with the snowdrifts, the landscape's awful queer.

"After some time, he hears a snatch of music on the wind. So he thinks he's so late, they've gone and got another fiddler. Well, there's nought for it but to keep heading for the music, so at least he'll be out of the cold. Soon he hears it again, awful close this time. But when he looks around, he canna see a thing. No lights frae the house or nothing. But there's the music again, coming out the side of a hill. And there's a little opening there in the hill, with light streaming out."

"They always go in," said Laurie.

"Aye, but whether it's magic or what, the story doesna say. But whatever the reason, Jones, he goes into the hill. And it's all shining like, the braaest hall you've ever seen. No lamps nor anything, just all glowing. And sure, it wasna just one fiddler playing, but a whole flock of them is at it, and ever so many folk dancing. They was trows, of course.

"But when Jones he comes in, all the fiddlers stop playing. This lassie though, she comes up to our man and hands him a mug of beer. And oh, she was a bonnie one. And Jones raises up his beer to toast her and is wondering at her being just the bonniest peerie lassie he's ever seen. She seems somehow familiar, but he canna quite place her. And when she leans over to whisper in his ear, well, it couldna be going better for him. But it's not sweet nothings she whispers. It's that he shouldna touch the drink, nor any of the meat in the place.

"It's what *learned* folk like yourself, Innes, calls a *taboo*. But it could just as well be common sense. I kens you young folk will drink with just anyone, but there's folk best avoided. For if our Jones here had taken just a sip of that beer, he'd have been lost forever. There's no coming back frae the trows if you've taken their meat or drink. And it's like that with some women too. So just you mind." John coughed lightly. "So anyway, this lassie tells him he has to play the fiddle. That's his only chance. He's to play the fiddle all night, right till sunrise, and when the very first rays of sun come in through the entrance to the hill, then he has to run.

"And these words, they scare that fiddle right into his hands, and he starts to play. All the trows is dancing. It was a sight to behold, these trows dancing up and down the floor of the hill. Jones, he plays and plays, but after a bit, it seems as the trows is getting weary frae all the dancing. Remember, they was dancing before he came. But he looks out through the door of the hill and sees it's still night."

"He'd have had it easier," said Laurie, "if you'd set the story in summer."

"My boy's a cynic," John said. "It's winter in this story, so morning's still a long way off. Without even pausing, Jones starts playing a reel, and he plays so furious, the trows has no choice but to dance. He keeps this up for hours, until he sees the first rays of light coming through the hole in the hill. As that light's coming in, the doorway's shrinking, getting narrower. He stops playing then, in the middle of a tune, and he just runs fast as he can through the hall and out the door. It's morning now, so the trows canna chase him, and by the time he's got a bit away and looks back, the hole's disappeared.

"In the morning light, he can see that the hill's Trollakeldas Houlla, which is famous for its trows, ken? And that's not so great a distance frae his own home at Mid-Yell. It's not so far as he walked the night before at least. But he goes home, and sure, there's all his neighbours, worried sick, for he'd not appeared at the party as planned.

"And they was all in his house, crying and wailing that he'd fallen over the cliffs or been buried in the snow. They'd been so sad, they'd drank all the gin in the house, even the bottle hid up in the rafters. And I tell you, Innes, that was the last time Jones ever went walking out in the dark with his fiddle."

John glanced at his son and coughed again. "Just played summer weddings after that."

I Have Not Answered

"That was wonderful," the young man said.

"Well," said John, "it wasn't as good as all that. I'm not a real storyteller. Graham's a real storyteller, he is."

★

I SAT IN THE ARMCHAIR, watching him sleep. The blanket slipped, baring his shoulder, and I wondered whether he had the consciousness to pull it back up. He gave a little kick, dragging the blanket farther down and exposing the whiteness of his thigh.

The night was still. Fog purled down Murnin Kame, would be piling up in the valley in the lee of the ridge. Here, it slid across the grass, dropping off the cliffs, into the sea.

I waited for him to dream. That is when one can see through their eyes. Though it is not straightforward. A few nights ago, he dreamt of apples, whatever that betokened. He was in a shop, choosing red and green apples and placing them in a bag held by a blonde woman. Maybe it was Sal.

Some dreams are more entertaining than others.

Yet the young man is nevertheless quite entertaining, if only because he is different from most of them. Every morning, and other times too, there is a curious thing he does. He will burn a little cone of that noxious something on his white flower plate. Then he seats himself upon the floor in a way that is very queer, rather like that little person in his jade knickknack. And so he sits on the floor in his underwear, his back straight and his feet atop their opposite thighs, palms facing up and knuckles meeting in his lap.

And he sits there like that for a long time. His eyes are closed, so you might think he was asleep. But when he opens his eyes and stands up, he is very alert and not the least bit drowsy. This is a curious thing he does.

I stopped looking at the young man and turned back to the paper in my lap. One of those letters. To Sal, I guess, but there was no name at the top. *I don't like the thought of you being lonely. I'll be home again before long once I get the story. Then we'll talk things through, if that'll do any good. I guess you haven't seen him since. I trust you. But sometimes I can't help wondering. I guess that makes me weak. You've always been the one I could trust and the one I couldn't see through. I can see through all the others, straight through to the other side. But it's part of why you're special to me. It gives me hope, loving someone I can't understand.*

I've always loved you. I'm always thinking of you.

Shortly after going to bed, he had got up again and written at the bottom of the page, *I'm thinking about you.*

Then he thought about her.

Quite vigorously, as it happens.

When he was done and had cleaned himself, he fell asleep. They rarely dream straight afterward. It is a quirk of the brain.

So the night was a weary one, and in my boredom, I thought about this place in South called *Uni*, where people go to learn about electricity and music and medicine and money and things. They also make books there, though I do not

I Have Not Answered

often find them interesting. However, as there was nothing else to do, I looked through the young man's Uni books.

One of them actually consisted of many different books all put together, and among these was a thing the likes of which I had never read before. There was a bit of it that struck me then and there: *Some men have told me they have seen a doubleman, or the shape of some man in two places; that is, a superterranean and a subterranean inhabitant, perfectly resembling one another in all points. They call this reflex-man a Co-Walker, every way like the man, as a twin-brother and companion, haunting him as his shadow, as is oft seen and known among men, both before and after the original is dead. This copy, echo, or living picture, goes at last to his own herd. It accompanied that person so long and frequently for ends best known to itself, whither to guard him from the secret assaults of some of its own folks, or only as a sportful ape to counterfeit all his actions.*

This was written by a minister called Robert Kirk, who lived in South many years ago. So struck was I by this passage, I resolved to take the book away to study at my leisure.

Just as this thought came to me, I heard a sort of scrabbling outside. I was not at all sure I had heard it, for the noise had come just as I snapped the book shut.

But there it was again.

I looked out the window behind the armchair.

Fog slid knee-deep over the ground, spilling off the cliffs.

Anything could have been hiding down in the fog, and you would not have known it.

Yet I sensed the thing was pressed up close against the wall, just beside the window. I could feel the chill of it on my right cheek. It took all my self-control not to turn and look.

For there are some you cannot see, and there are others you would not want to see for the horror of it.

But if I remained very still, perhaps it would creep out toward the window and look at me.

And then maybe it would see through me as through a pane of frosted glass, or maybe it would perish at the horror of me. I cannot say. One cannot see oneself through another's eyes.

The thing outside must have thought something similar, for I heard its body grind against the wall as it slid into the fog. It left a wake in the fog as it zigzagged off toward the cliffs.

I was just about to leave the cottage myself when an image came into my head from the sleeping young man's dream eyes. There spread out before me close-crowded granite buildings. A woman in white trousers and a blue jumper walked toward him, halting and stiff, like a wading bird. She carried her head bent, and blonde hair obscured her face so I could not tell if it was same woman from the dream with the apples.

But he ran toward her, reached out, and held her tight, his head over her shoulder. Someone was sobbing. He hugged her even tighter, and it was then I marked an uncanny thing, though I did not yet discern its particularity. But the woollen jumper stretched as he slid a hand down her back, and it occurred to me that even as he held her close, there was no warmth to her. He slid his hand farther down and cupped it around a buttock. Clasping tighter still, he squeezed.

Her trousers cracked and peeled like old white paint, and part of her came away in his hand, crumbling to grey grit. He held her tight as he could, seeking to hold her together. But this was a mistake, for under the pressure, she broke down entirely and became a heap of grit on the pavement, with blonde hair lying alongside. A roar of wind rounded the corner and charged the narrow street, blowing the dust and gravel away—out and away, I thought. Out to the sea.

The young man woke with a gasp and a shudder. He sat bolt upright in bed.

A funny dream, that.

"Sal?" he whispered. He did not look around the room. I suppose he knew she was not there. "Sal."

Holding the book close to my body, I left him for the night.

★

THE YOUNG MAN was in Walls interviewing the Methodist minister, a man whose words I cannot abide.

Something very like boredom possessed me as I made for the spine of Murnin Kame. From up the ridge, the west was all drowned in sea, lochs and hillocks dappled the east, and Sumburgh Head rose far to the south. Heather flowered purple all around. They have written songs about that, you know.

Whenever I stand here, I sense this place was once my

home. It is a vague feeling. The need for a home dissipates with the ages as one's people scatter and turn to dust. But it must have been very long ago, if indeed it ever was.

I do not dream. Yet there are pictures sometimes, coming and going, bleeding out into time, the eternal present, which is so long. Then you wake and do not remember where you are or where you were. If you recall who you are, it is a failure of the imagination. You are never anything to yourself.

And the world is so vast all around.

Down below, a little car made its way out of Walls. I knew the car to be that of Laurie Millar. He bought it down in Aberdeen some three or four years since. Whether it was constructed in Aberdeen, I cannot say. Some of them are made in a place called *Japan*, which is a far off place in South where people kill one another with swords, eat nothing but raw fish bundled up in rice, and fly aeroplanes into boats. How a people that has not learned to cook fish can nevertheless construct cars, I do not dare venture, yet there must be some among them more technically capable than the rest. But anyway.

Laurie's car stopped at the village shop in the lee of the ridge. The shop is open just four days a week and does not even have a jar of hard coloured candy on the counter. But it does have tins and things, and Bill drives out to the bakery in Walls for bannocks, rolls, and sliced bread. He goes to town once a week too to pick up special items, like apples.

Now they have high-speed broadband, smartphones, and wind turbines. But things never really change, not in any essential way. It is a pretence of theirs that change is rushing past them and that they are all living in a new world, yet I cannot recall it ever having been otherwise. The Picts, in their time, thought they were living in a new world too, and the Northmen and the Scots after that.

This morning, the young man had been talking to himself. They often talk to themselves after having stayed alone for a time. A lack of human contact, I suppose, the need to hear a voice from across the table or a breath in bed beside them. Most speak to themselves as if they were another, completing the illusion of fellowship by calling themselves *you*. The most violent arguments are between one person's various *you*s.

Men are pitiable creatures. I do not envy them in the slightest. It is easy, by contrast, for we who scarcely are to know the measure of our own being. Not for me, the anxiety of the ephemeral. I have always the boundless past and future, and if I am thus always alone, it is a state of peace, like a rock in the ocean. I am no less material than they, but my materiality is of a different sort, woven from a coarser fabric or sculpted from a more pure clay, as the metaphor demands.

Most first begin talking to themselves after some weeks, but the young man did it from the start. Maybe he was alone before he came here. Their passions are so base that even one such as I, who has studied them so long, cannot fully understand.

While washing up in the kitchen this morning, the young man had said, "She's like a flower. You love her like a beautiful flower. But his head's on the pillow beside her. You made her tell you precisely what happened, everything they did. You thought it would help. Honesty. Everything out in the open."

Then he frowned, inhaled deeply, and said, "The lotus rises from the mud of desire and blossoms unstained."

The metaphors they demand are different from my own.

He went into the main room, lit his cone thing, and sat on the floor with his legs crossed. This time, the fumes ached my head more than usual, and I was compelled to leave him.

★

THE YOUNG MAN half dozed on the sand in the nook of the narrow inlet. He had spent the morning conducting interviews. After so much coffee and biscuits during his visits, his head must have been buzzing from the hospitality.

The wind bit in the fields above, but the sun shone strong, and the summer chill was not so severe down in the shelter of the inlet. His eyes were closed. I suspect he was listening to the broken waves pulling back from the shore.

Out in the sea, the waves reformed and cast themselves again upon the sands, as doomed whales intent on beaching for ends best known to themselves. Had his eyes been open, he would have seen the sea through the gap in the cliffs. Foula reclined there above the waters, half dozing too in pretence of peace.

A dream image flickered before me, on and off. It seemed a party of some sort. I heard a snatch of music and saw a blonde-haired woman holding a beer.

I Have Not Answered

Then the image was gone.

I once again saw the world as it was, through the entrance to the inlet, Foula lording over.

The young man yawned.

Another image came, now of the same woman holding a fiddle. It was gone again in an instant.

These mere specks of dreams. One is left unsatisfied. I should have liked to have heard the woman play. What would she have played? 'Da Farder Ben da Welcomer', I imagined. But then, why should she play a Shetland song? One of those songs they play in South. Play guitar and sing 'Barbara Allen' perhaps. Yes, 'Barbara Allen'. I could imagine that.

The young man moaned.

There was a skittering of stones down the side of the inlet. The young man and I looked up as one.

At first, I thought it was one of them. Then I saw her sturdy old brown boots and knew it was not.

A young woman, May Stevens, came down the natural steps in the rock and onto the beach. She looked at the young man, then at the sea, and back again. "Tide's coming in."

He roused himself and leapt up rather awkwardly.

"Water will be up past the steps in half an hour. And it's no the weather for swimming."

He opened and closed his mouth dumbly. From his angle, Foula – hazy and distant – haloed the woman's slender face and short black hair. He looked dizzy or disoriented, and he placed a hand against the rock wall for support.

She did not move. "Innes, yeah? I'm May. Margaret's daughter."

He nodded, but still he could not speak.

She stepped to the side and leaned back against the cliff face. He followed her with his head, and Foula slipped out of sight. Her dark green jacket was rugged and worn, practical.

His speech returned. "You're at Uni in Glasgow?"

"Second year engineering. And I hear du's doing a degree in trowies. But I guess du has another name for it."

"Folklore. A PhD in Folklore."

Out over the Atlantic, storm clouds were gathering. I saw the fey streamers go up over Foula, first as white threads twisting out of the turf, then as blood ribbons writhing like snakes. They went slack an instant before being picked up on the wind and carried off to fulfil their fates across the waters.

May's face glowed white against the black rock. "How long is du in Shetland?"

"It's hard to say. I'll be here till I get what I need."

"And what are dy needs, then?"

The young man thought a moment. "I need to find a story."

"Du'll have no trouble there."

"A particular story."

"What story is it?"

"I can't tell you." He hesitated. "I have to avoid prompting. People often repeat what they've been told. It doesn't help me if I make people remember something they never knew to begin with. So I just have to wait until someone tells it to me."

I Have Not Answered

"I see."

"I'm patient. Really, I just need to find out if the story has a happy ending or a sad ending."

"Which ending do you want?"

"I can't tell you that either."

★

IT DOES NOT DO to get involved. They live so short a time. Besides, there is danger in it.

But this one is interesting. He is unlike the others, and I thought I might perhaps help him in some way. All this time, and still he had not met Graham Stevens. It is a funny thing, but I felt a bit sorry for him.

To miss Graham Stevens was no great loss. But neither had the young man known Graham's father. And Paul Stevens had been one worth remembering. When he told stories, even those such as I sometimes came to listen. When he was old, he would sit in his chair in front of the television, his back to the screen, and tell stories whether the children would listen or not. When he was young though, well, then they would all gather together, women at their knitting, men fixing up hooks and nets, peat reek from the fire.

There's tunnels under all the islands, Paul said. *Islands is riddled with them. Maybe under where we's sitting now. Most of them's hollowed out by waves coming into the cliffs. No mystery. But there's some as we dunna ken where they goes or where they's frae. And so there's one just under where we's sitting now. And du can come in by boat down at the bottom of these cliffs.*

But it's no the sea's hollowed it.

No.

'Cause this tunnel.

It goes straight through.

But it doesna come out the other side.

Just keeps going a place farther than any man can tell.

But there's one man tried and tell it.

He's a fiddler, see? Plays the fiddle. Man says, 'Going into tunnel, seeing where it is.' Says he'll play as he goes, so his friends up top can hear. Hear the fiddle through the rock. And when he's going, he'll play a brisk tune. And when he's stopping, he'll play a slow one. So when they hear it slow, they'll ken where the tunnel ends. Hear him up through the rock. Then he'll come back, he will.

So the man goes down the cliffs, into the tunnel. All he's with him is his fiddle, a light to see with, and his peerie white dog. And he goes and is playing brisk. His friends follow right across the hills, till they's out past Neuglesbreck. Tune's nice and cheery to hear.

Then it's changed.

But it's no playing slow.

Playing mad, something fearful. Music's all in a mess. Then stops. And doesna start again.

And so, the men, they run back as they came and row out to the start of the tunnel. Dunna waste any time.

And that little white dog, it's hopping there on the rocks.

Hopping and jabbering like mad.

I Have Not Answered

No wonder. Fur's all burned off. Its fur's been burned off. Dog stinks of sulphur, see? And scratches on its haunch, as from claws.

Never found what's happened to their friend. The fiddler.

And never been another so brave or so stupid as would enter that tunnel since.

I do not often think of Paul Stevens. The old days are old and are of no use to me. But when I think of Paul Stevens, it is with a sort of fondness. So I felt sorry for the young man and wanted to help.

This day, the young man had packed himself a fine lunch. A couple of bannocks from the bakery in Walls, a big red apple, a hunk of farmhouse cheddar, and an odd little sausage wrapped up in fiddly plastic. I enjoyed his lunch immensely.

Visitors must plan their meals ahead when they are out in the country. Only a local will know whether the shop or pub will be open at any given time and whether they will be able to sell you something even if they are. I was aware the young man was interviewing Conrad Neely in Sandness in the morning. I also knew that Hermaneuk Inn would be open for lunch, catering chiefly to the handful of late-summer visitors taking part in one of the Papa Stour Nature Tours.

It was not until the young man reached Melby Beach and rooted around in his rucksack that he realised his food was gone. His lunch bag now held a piece of driftwood and some tufts of wool that I had collected from the fence at Finnigarth.

He held these things, turned them over in his hand, and peered around the beach as though he expected someone to be watching. Papa lay innocuously across the sound, and I nearly laughed aloud when he looked in that direction too.

He rubbed the wool between his fingers and sniffed it. Whether he is in the habit of sniffing wool, I cannot say, but I have never seen him do so before despite an abundance of opportunity. He stood up, only to stoop down again and take everything out of his rucksack quite methodically, emptying all the little pockets. He set the carrying case with his audio recorder onto the sand, then his fieldnotes, pocket calendar, Ordnance Survey map, and four ballpoint pens all in a row. He stared at these things a moment. Then, very resolutely, without a glance in either direction, he repacked his rucksack. He even replaced the driftwood and wool in the bag, which is odd since I cannot imagine what use he might have for them.

Looking straight ahead as he went, he walked off the beach and across the field to his bicycle at Gord. I could not, of course, keep up with him on the bicycle, but I followed after as best I could, cutting across the fields. When I came up out of Shen Dale, I saw the bicycle leaning against the side of Hermaneuk Inn, just as I had planned.

By the time I got inside, the young man had already ordered: lamb with mint sauce and chips, it turned out. Every dish at Hermaneuk Inn comes with chips. They are shipped up frozen from town and shipped to town on the North Boat.

The young man stood at the bar with a pint of ale. He was chatting with Florrie, who was working, and Henry from Norby, who was sipping a Tennent's and half-reading yesterday's paper. The young man is very good at chatting. He smiles at all the right times, asks questions about sheep, and never lets on if he is bored. Even I cannot always tell when he is bored. I imagine those who speak with him feel for a moment that they are at the centre of someone else's universe.

The young man was buying a drink for Henry. He twisted around on the barstool and tried to catch the attention of a man sitting in the corner booth, staring at an empty glass.

"Have a drink?" the young man called out.

Henry huffed, and Florrie said, "He'll not refuse, if you're offering." She poured out a measure of cheap whisky.

The young man crossed over to the booth and set the whisky on the table. He extended his hand. "Innes Pitmedden."

The man looked up. His white beard, nurtured by neglect, was shaved off every few weeks as the spirit possessed him. He pulled the whisky over and settled his blue eyes upon the glass, rubbing a thick, tobacco-stained finger against the rim.

The young man shifted on his feet. He seemed to want an excuse to return to the bar. "Well," he said, "I'd better..."

"Aye."

The young man hesitated. "Fine weather."

"Aye."

"You live in Sandness?"

The man did not look up.

Florrie behind the bar seemed torn whether to intervene.

This unwonted opposition sparked something in the young man. He sat down at the booth.

The young man is a seeker of the truth, and he will have it regardless of whether it wants to be found. I love him for his guile and ruthlessness. "Things," he said, "are not as they were."

The man did not look up. "No, that's right enough."

"They were different before the oil."

"Oh, aye. There's the oil."

"Changed everything," the young man said.

Henry called over, "But they'd have changed regardless, you know. Couldn't live in the past forever."

The young man ignored him. "Some things are worse, others better."

"There's the roads," the man said.

"But the fishing," the young man said, "that's a sorry thing."

"It's not as it was."

"Were you in the fishing?"

The man looked up, wary. "And then the fish farming."

"It's not a bad business."

"Man wasna meant to be pulling salmon out of a cage."

"Well, that's the times, isn't it?"

"That's all I'm saying." The man rose, gulped down his whisky, then hobbled out of the pub.

Florrie set down a plate of lamb with mint sauce and chips as the young man reclaimed his barstool. Cocking her head in the direction of the door, she said, "Don't take it personally. Like that with everyone, is our Graham."

★

I Have Not Answered

At nine o'clock the next morning, the young man was seated in the Stevens' kitchen, with a basic Shetland visitor's map from the tourist office spread out before him. His Ordnance Survey map lay on the writing table in the cottage.

Margaret pointed at the map. "Follow the road out of Walls, then take the left toward Gruting. Staneydale Temple's signposted from there."

"Sounds simple."

"Oh, you'll find it, surely."

He sipped at his coffee. "By the way. I met your husband yesterday at Hermaneuk Inn."

Margaret blanched, but the young man had the good manners not to be watching.

His manners are indeed very fine. Most people's politeness is limited in scope. But this young man, he is like one of those lizards with horns on its head that you see in books. It is not that he changes colour. Nor is it the case that all of them have horns. But anyway. He is like them in that he changes to suit his company. I have heard him talking engine repair, mermaids, agricultural policy.

Margaret said, "You met May the other day, didn't you?"

The young man looked down at the table.

"She's out with the sheep now. If you'd like to—"

"Actually, I'd love to talk with Graham again."

Margaret rifled pointlessly through some papers on the counter. "Well, you'll have to ask Graham about that, of course."

"So many people have told me that he knows some stories."

"Oh, he does that, yes."

"That he knows things."

They heard the front door open.

Margaret brightened. "That'll be May now."

May breezed into the kitchen, hung her wet jacket on the chair beside the young man, and turned directly to the counter to pour some coffee from the pot.

"Innes was just saying about you," said Margaret.

"Hmm-mm," said May.

"Well..." The young man began to fold up his map.

May placed her hand in the middle of the map and sat beside him. "Where's du going the day?" She peeked under where her hand had, by chance, landed. "Vidlin? Ach, man. There's nought in Vidlin du canna find here in the Westside."

"He's for Staneydale, May." Shaking her head, Margaret left the room.

May raised an eyebrow. "Du'll be studying all wir native antiquities and ancient relics. We'll need to be building some new ones before du runs out of what's already here."

The young man finished folding up the map. "It's mainly the stories surrounding them that interest me." He tried standing, but May gripped his forearm and held him in place.

"I kens a story about Staneydale. I'll tell it to dee while du finishes dy coffee." She took her mug in both hands and raised it to her lips.

The young man gazed at her lips. Then he realised what he was doing and looked into her blue eyes instead.

"It was many a year ago," May said, "and there's this crofter living in West Houlland. And it comes time to take the sheep in frae the hills. But when he's rounded up the flock, he sees an awful number of them is missing. Not just the usual sorts of numbers frae cold and sickness. And there hadna been any big storms lately either. So it's very queer, this with the sheep.

"So. This man, he thinks as maybe some of these sheep has moved down inta Staneydale, and he'll go take a look. But though the day had started clear, it's got awful foggy like. But go he must, just to make certain. As he's walking inta the dale, this fog, it gets thicker and thicker. Soon, it's all he can do to see his ain hand in front of him, and he's stumbling over rocks and falling and everything, completely disoriented.

"But he canna just stand there. He has to do something. So he keeps walking till he sees the outline of Staneydale Temple in the fog. And Staneydale's an uncanny place even when the sun's shining, so in the fog it seems something terrible. And then he sees these queer shapes moving over the ground. Almost floating like. Nor is it just one or two of them, but all numbers. And this crofter, he thinks back on the tales he's heard about Staneydale and all the trowies that dwell there. He's thinking his end has come, for if there's one thing the trowies dunna like, it's being seen by mortal eyes.

"And when some of these shapes starts coming at him, he just drops down to his knees, and he starts praying. He's never been a praying man before, but now's as good a time as any, so he starts praying, 'Lord, preserve me frae these trowies' and all that. But when next he looks up, he kens his prayer hasna been heard, for these figures, well, some of them's just a few yards off. And he's terrified, yeah? So he just shuts tight his eyes. And a moment later, he can feel their hot breath on his face, kneeling down as he is, and then—"

May paused for effect. The young man was smiling wryly.

"And then. One of these things comes right up and rubs its big wet nose in his face and says 'Baaaa.' And so that's what'd become of his sheep. And that explains the trowies." May put down her mug. "Has du heard that one before?"

He shrugged. "Well, you know, that kind of story— It doesn't really say anything about belief in trows, does it? I mean, don't get me wrong, you know. But these stories didn't all come from people mistaking sheep in the fog. It's deeper than that. It's human nature. It's like we need to believe in things, need to experience them."

May winked at him. "It's just a story."

"I mean, but..." He was seeking words he did not have.

"Does du no like stories then?"

He straightened his back and set his face. "I don't know that I particularly like stories. Whether I like stories isn't the issue. I'm interested in what stories have to say. And that story you just told says that people are so confused by the fact that people used to believe in trows that they have to make up humorous stories to explain it."

"What does a *real* trowie story say then?"

"It says people believed they had experiences with trows."

"Aye, aye, I hear dee," May said sceptically. She tapped a finger atop one of his hands resting on the table. "So it's du what gets to choose which stories mean something other than what they say and which stories actually mean what they say."

"Well," he said, "if you're offering."

"Du's the professional?"

"Can't let the natives to decipher their own customs. It requires expertise. Training. Take your language for instance."

"Is my dialect no good enough for dee?"

"What do you speak down in Glasgow? English, right? But of course, you're not really speaking dialect to me either. That's not how you'd speak to your mother if you two were alone. Or to Laurie. If you two were alone."

The young man eyed her blush rather clinically, which seemed to displease her.

"What you speak to me is a bastardised dialect. It's neither the one thing nor the other. You're trying to make three points. One is that dialect is important to you. Another is that it's important for outsiders to know dialect is important to you. And third, you think I couldn't understand real dialect. In fact, it's insulting."

"If du's so easily insulted…"

He hesitated, as if rolling new words around in his mouth. An odd look came over his face. "With the dialect, you're like a chameleon. You change colours to match your surroundings. You're insecure and never know who you are. But not even a chameleon can change the colour of its horns."

It is strange how people struggle for mastery, as if any of their actions mattered, as if, once achieved, their mastery would be eternal. As if they themselves were forever. Some of them, I am aware, actually do believe their souls will live forever. Whether this belief is true, I have no way of knowing. But I am inclined to doubt it.

The stories they tell about trows and such, these at first confused me, for much of it I did not recognise. Then it occurred to me that they have these stories the wrong way about. They place their own passions in the minds of others, try to make all living things think as they do.

"All right then," said May. "I'll tell dee another story, yeah?"

The young man nodded. I am certain he would have preferred to leave so he could go out and interview old people, but this is a part of his nature he cannot alter.

"This story isna about trowies. It's no even about trowies that aren't trowies. It means exactly what it says. It's about selkies. Kens du what's selkies?"

He said nothing, then realised she was waiting for an answer. "Seals."

"Aye, seals. But back then, folk said not all seals was alike. There was seals, and then there was selkies. Seals is just harbour seals. The peerie ones, ken? Selkies is all the big sorts, like grey seals and that. And seals is just seals. But selkies is something magic. Thing about selkies is, if they wanted, they could turn inta people. They'd these skins, ken? Which they could take off when they was ashore. Then they'd be just like people.

I Have Not Answered

"Well, there's once this man walking down the beach, gathering limpets. And he's walking down the beach when he sees ahead of him these nine lasses dancing. And they're all naked. Not a shred on them, ken? And he creeps up, creeps up so's they canna see him. And soon he's right up close to them. And they're just dancing away like.

"Well, these are all real stunners. But there's one lass what's so bonnie as would break dy heart to see her, Innes. It really would. She's this lovely shiny black hair and just the whitest skin and eyes so deep as du canna imagine. So this man, now he's got up close, he can see these selkie skins lying on the rocks. And he's well aware what kind of women these are. But they really are just so bonnie, he canna help it. So up he jumps and grabs the skin nearest him. And these lasses, well, they snatch up their skins, leap inta the water, and turn back inta selkies.

"All except one, of course, what canna do it as this man has got her skin. And of course, it's the particularly bonnie lass with black hair what's been left behind. And so she begs this man, pleads for her skin back, else she canna return to the sea and be with her ain kind.

"But this man. He's no a bad man precisely, but he's a man for all that, and he just doesna have it in him to let her go. So he says, 'Du's best come hame with me, love, and I'll make a wife of dee so's it's all proper.' This lass, she doesna want to go, but she's really no choice, seeing as she canna return to the sea. So she goes with him, and they get married.

"But these days being as they is, before condoms and the pill and that, it's no time at all before this man and his selkie wife have seven bairns. And this husband, he loves his wife ever so dearly, dotes on her, ken? But she doesna reciprocate, and it's often as she'll be sad and crying.

"And sometimes, she goes down to the beach and stands there crying inta the sea. And a great big bull selkie will stick his snout up frae the water and bellow at her, and they'll start what sounds like a conversation, all in selkie talk.

"Well, there's this one day the husband's away at the fishing, and this wife is alone with their seven bairns. She's in the house when these bairns, in they run, all excited, and the oldest is saying he's found something in the barn, a fine selkie skin, and it was in a little chest hid under a load of straw. And he holds up the skin to show to his mother. She recognises it, naturally, as her ain skin. And she snatches the skin frae him, kisses her bairns farewell, and runs off toward the beach.

"It's just a minute later, the husband, he gets home and finds the bairns crying. And the oldest, he just about manages to tell how he'd found this selkie skin. And the man, he kens what's up, so off he dashes down to the beach as fast he can.

"But he's too late. He reaches the beach just as his wife slips back inta her skin and leaps inta the sea as a selkie. And up bobs this bonnie selkie head frae the water, and up bobs the head of this great bull selkie beside her. And it's 'I loved dee well enough,' she says to the man, 'and may all good attend dee. But I always loved my first husband much better.'

I Have Not Answered

And cry though he might, she wouldna come ashore again but just swimmed off with her mate.

"So," said May, "has du heard that one before?"

"I have."

"But never has du heard it told so sweet."

The young man was jittery as he walked home.

I could not understand it. He had forgotten about Graham, and the visit had been a waste. As it was, he would probably feel obligated to visit Staneydale anyway, just to save face.

They are strange, the way they think. One thing leads to another, with no connection in between.

★

LONG AGO, when the people first came in their little boats, there was forest here. Men's tools and animals removed the trees, which had impeded their mastery of the land. When at last the islands were barren, wind could sweep the land unimpeded, and nature removed men's mastery once more.

If you stand at Eshaness, as I sometimes do, you will perhaps find it difficult to imagine. Boulders and tiny brown lochs on a glacier-stripped plain. Time was, people worshipped these boulders and lochs, offering them prayer and sacrifice. At the cliffs, the land has been torn away in great hunks, and seabirds breed and die and defecate on its unhealing wounds.

It is not many generations since they built a lighthouse here. From its tower, you can see all the way out to nothing in the west. You can see this nothing just as well from the cliffs themselves. They say the lighthouse is to protect boats, but I do not believe it, for the Picts built a broch tower here too, yet there were no boats from the west to protect in their time. Maybe they gain a sense of mastery from it, projecting their vain light over the waters.

Close beside the lighthouse is a long, deep cut in the plain, called Calder's Geo. At the bottom of the geo lies a heap of boulders, cast onto the beach by the sea. There is a cave down there, and it connects by secret paths to tunnels that run throughout the islands. There are things at Calder's Geo that say it is here the tunnels start and here the digging of them commenced long ago, yet the things of Folga Skerry off Papa claim the same honour, and I am not at all certain which of them to believe. I am inclined to suspect that the tunnels are from the time of those who came before. But as there is no glory in such an assertion, it goes largely unsaid.

In the summer, tourists spill out from their coaches to look down over the cliffs. They joke about falling, invariably, and the sheerness of it is a game for them.

Though I have witnessed storms here so strong as to push sheep and even cows across the slipping moss and over the cliffs, their carcasses never to be recovered by men.

And when the tourists are done, they visit Tangwick Haa museum, which tells about life in the old days and gives them a chance to buy coffee and biscuits. They have already had coffee – and perhaps soup, sandwiches, and cake as well – at

I HAVE NOT ANSWERED

Braewick Café on the way to Eshaness. So by the end of it, their corporeal requirements really are altogether sated. I do not begrudge them this. I just think it worth mentioning.

But anyway. The young man biked out to Eshaness in stages, overnighting in Brae and stopping in Hillswick. He jotted down details about the landscape in his book of fieldnotes. I could see his heart was not in it. What it all had to do with his search for a story, I do not know. I suspect it was merely industry for industry's sake. Like the digging of the tunnels perhaps.

The day was grey and the sky unbroken. Foula lay hidden in the sea fog, beyond the reach of the keenest eye, but the young man strained for it anyway.

I could not imagine what he wanted to see there. It unsettled me.

I do not, as a rule, care much about them in their particularity. They are part of the landscape, like the sheep, the dry stone dykes, the otters. This one though, he has something foreign about him. He watches and observes, speaks without saying anything, responds without answering. He would be a mirror for the rest of them, should they one day learn to see. And like a mirror, nothing he reflects leaves a mark or impresses itself upon him. Like me, he is unchanging and unmoved, though he has contrived to mimic the speech of men in their turmoil and amuses himself with it sometimes while alone. "You've always loved her. She's a flower," and so on. A poorer observer than I might believe his thoughts are like those of the others. I know this is just practice. That is why he only says these things when no one is listening.

The ground dropped off directly before his feet. A tourist would be looking down, but he stared out toward hidden Foula, his eyes drawn by a pull coming through the fog.

"We travel along the Six Paths, flowing from jealousy to suffering to wilful contentment. But the circle is unbroken."

He flung a pebble down over the cliff. It disappeared from sight long before it hit the water.

"What's love anyway? You're beyond all that. It diverts you from enlightenment. It's weakness. Banish your will by banishing your desire. Banish your desire by banishing your passion. There's a science to it, an intricate causality. It is law. When you feel as if you're being watched, that's the gaze of Kanzeon, Bosatsu of Compassion, she who observes the lamentations of the world, beckoning you to deathlessness."

It is queer, but when he and I are apart, I feel a kind of emptiness, as though something were missing. So I have taken keepsakes: a Uni book, some strands of hair, a half-written letter to Sal. He is my reflection, my shadow. I do not touch him. I leave no mark. This mirroring changes nothing.

But were all things otherwise, I should like to have cared for him as I would have cared for myself.

There has never been anyone to care for me.

Nor do I require care. Like a rock in the ocean, I am still. Like the string of a harp unplayed.

Yet he is only a man. He is fragile and not forever.

I Have Not Answered

But do you know? Last night I caught a glimpse of a face shining up at me and a smile sweet and sorrowful as the music of a harp. It must have been through the young man's dream eyes, I am sure of it, though it felt somehow different.

For when I think of it now, the memory is all subtle and diffuse, a fine mist in place of where my soul would be, if I had a soul. I tried to focus on that face, and the vision fell away, bleeding out into the darkness of the room around me.

★

THE YOUNG MAN was at Hermaneuk Inn, sharing a table with John and Laurie Millar. May Stevens sat by Laurie's side. The rounds of beer had turned full circle, as had the conversation: a new couple who had moved to Walls, computers at the Council, the roads on Papa, endless trivialities.

Yet the young man was watching May more than the rest. He was studying her.

In the midst of the conversation, John cleared his throat. "Well, now. I've a story for our folklorist." He took a sip of beer then cleared his throat again.

"And here we were, getting on," Laurie said.

"The boy's come up from Aberdeen," John said.

Laurie rolled his eyes.

Without awaiting further protest, John began. "Well. You'll have heard of the smuggling?"

The young man nodded.

John slipped into a light dialect. "There was a time when full on half the Shetland men had a hand in the smuggling. It was all frae gin to timber to meal to tea, coming in frae Holland. And so the Customs House was down in Fort Charlotte in town. All the excisemen was English or Scots. Most was English, for them in London didna trust a Scot any more than us. And it goes without saying, you couldna get a Shetlander to do the job.

"Well, there's come a new man to head the Customs House. This must've been about one hundred and fifty years since. And he's come up frae London or wherever, and he has a talk with these excisemen. He canna fathom how there could be so much smuggling on one small little flock of islands that's home to so many excisemen. It just didna make sense.

"Well, next time it's being said a big illicit cargo's being landed— this is round about Fladdabister, in the south. Next night it happens, what this Customs Master does, he gets all his excisemen and gathers as many soldiers frae the Fort as he can, and off they troop to where this boat's meant to be coming in. And sure, there's a whole load of Shetland lads hauling barrels of gin and crates of tea and whatnot up off the beach. So these soldiers and these excisemen, they descend on the smugglers. The Shetland lads is a bit shocked, ken? For it was a muckle queer thing, this: The excisemen had never been kent to trouble themselves over smuggling. And I dunna ken what it was what threw the first punch, but one way or another, both sides starts having it out with their fists and

I Have Not Answered

whatever bits of stuff is handy. It ends with casualties on both sides. And this new man what's in charge of the Customs House, he gets it worse than any. A barrel of gin's heaved up against his head, and he just falls down on the spot.

"He wakes next day, and sure, his head's aching something terrible. But worse is, his men, they tell him what's come of last night's raid. For they and the soldiers had fled the scene and been lucky to carry the Customs Master back with them. When they'd gone back in the morning, all the cargo was gone. Not a drop of gin left in Fladdabister. Shetland lads has always been thorough when it comes to putting away the spirits.

"But it wasna all bad news, for the night before, when the excisemen and soldiers had runned off, they'd managed to take one of the smugglers with them. And he was just a boy, ken? Fourteen, fifteen, that age. A local boy, here frae the Westside, though he was biding in Lerwick at the time. And I'll not say his name, for there's some of his folk still live in these parts. But catched him, they did, and they was holding him down at the Fort.

"And this was a real find, see? For the thing with these smugglers is, they'd never tell about one another if they was catched. Code of honour. And because these excisemen and soldiers was all foreigners, they didna ken the Shetland lads by sight. They'd no idea what they'd had this muckle battle with the night before. Except this boy. And you can be sure, this Customs man, he was just boiling. I dunna ken what they threatened over this boy, but in the end, he goes and tells the names of some of the folk what'd been in the fight."

Laurie and May both muttered. The young man was silent.

"And so the boy's released, and some men frae Lerwick and Cunningsburgh is arrested, and one of them's hanged. And you can be certain this boy didna sleep easy after that. It wasna just his conscience bothering him. He kenned well the punishment for telling the names of smugglers.

"And so he's moved back to his parents here in the Westside. That's the house you're biding in now, Innes, though it looked different back then. And so, late one night, when his folks is out of the house, there's this knocking at the door. This boy, he kens what's knocking, for here in Shetland, folk never knocked on doors in the old days. They just walked right in. So this knocking, it means something formal. It's his conscience, I guess, makes him open the door. It was a relief, maybe. But however it was, that's the last was kenned of him."

"Serves him right," Laurie said.

"Well though. It happened, years ago now, back when I was a boy, that Paul Stevens, what owned the house at the time, he's after putting in a new floor. It was a big thing then, in the '60s, putting in linoleum floors. But so he's cleared away the old flooring, and he finds a sort of trap door down beneath it, over by the door to the house. And he's curious, so he opens it, takes a torch, and drops down inta this peerie cellar. It wasna uncommon to have a sort of rude cellar in the old days to hide things that maybe you didna want found.

"So Paul is down in this cellar, just a couple of yards across and just so high as you can crouch in it. And he sees a jumble of bones back against the wall. And he's heard this story, so he kens straight off what's bones they is. And out he climbs from that cellar and covers it with the new flooring. For he kens, if he tells about it, sure, the Council will investigate, and the police will take a look, and it'll be a week before he can put down that floor. So he doesna tell."

Laurie asked, "How is it you found out then?"

"Well," said John, "after some years, and once his son had growed a bit up, he telled Graham about it. And it's Graham's telled me. I dunna suppose there's any harm in telling it further now, after so much time's passed. Though I suppose that boy's bones are lying there still."

"You never told me that story before," said Laurie.

The tale was now over, and John switched back out of dialect. "You never asked, boy. And besides, you're not after hearing stories about Shetland like our Innes."

"He wants to hear about trowies," said May.

"I'm interested in everything, really," Innes said.

"That must be nice." May placed her hand in Laurie's.

The young man took a drink.

"Will you sing, May? A song for Innes?" John said.

Laurie said, "We're not so far gone as all that?"

"No," said May, "we're not. Even though a great man from South is here to study wir customs. But as he's interested in everything and won't admit he only cares about trowies..."

Laurie removed his hand from May's, placing it in his lap.

"Does *du* have a song?" May asked the young man. "Or is du completely useless?"

For a moment, he did not answer. Then, "I have a song."

"Grand," said John. "That's grand."

"A Danish ballad called 'Agnete and the Merman'." The young man returned May's hard look. "It's a cautionary tale."

His singing voice was not good, but it was practical. He knows how music works but seems unaffected by it.

Agnete walks along the strand,
The merman comes and takes her hand.
"Hear now, Agnete, to what I say:
Will you be my sweet love this day?"

"Oh, so gladly that will I be,
If you take me into the sea."
He's plugged her mouth, he's plugged her ears,
He's taken her to the deep waters.

There they've lived seven long years,
Seven of the fairy's sons she rears.
By the cradle, Agnete sings,
Up above, the church bells ring.

Agnete asks the merman grey,
"May I go to church this day?"

I HAVE NOT ANSWERED

"Oh, yes, my dear, but please take care,
You mustn't let down your golden hair.

"And when you come on the church floor,
You mustn't go to your dear mother.
And when the priest does the Lord avow,
You mustn't your fair body bow."

Agnete's let down her golden hair,
She's walked up to her dear mother.
And when the priest did the Lord avow,
So deep, so deep down did she bow.

"Long you've shared the merman's bed,
How paid he for your maidenhead?"
"He's given to me this gold chalice,
That I may drink and feel sweet bliss.

"He's given to me this harp of gold,
That I may play when sorrowful."
Then in strode the merman bold,
And his eyes, his eyes were sorrowful.

"Hear now, Agnete, to what I say:
Your bairns, they cry for you this day."
"Let them cry, cry all they can,
For no more will I see them again."

The merman's taken her into the sea,
Her bonny bairns have torn her in three.
Her skull's their cup, her hand's their comb,
Her ribs' their harp when they're sorrowful.

Gruesome though the song was, it stirred something in me. It was really too horrible to contemplate.

Sometimes, I feel so queer and disconnected. Perhaps there are two worlds, like the reflection in a loch and the hills around.

And these two worlds, they never meet.

But then a storm whips up the waters, and it is possible to be confused, not know where the loch ends and the hillside begins.

"That's some song, man," Laurie said politely.

"If you walk with devils," the young man said, "you die with them. The woman died because she gave in to her passions. She lacked self-control. The merman was a demon, but he couldn't harm her without her consent."

"The Professor speaks," said May.

"Just because I know what I'm talking about, doesn't mean I'm not right." He paused. "Actually, the story I'm looking for in Shetland is a bit like that. Do you know anything along those lines?"

No one answered. The young man waited.

May said, "I thought du werena meant to tell wis what story du's after."

"Oh, that was just hint. It's not the same story. Just a bit similar. It's all completely justifiable as far as methodology is concerned. There's no harm in hinting."

★

I DO NOT INTEND to give the impression that Shetland is all countryside. There are little villages here and even a place people call *town*. They speak of towns in South too, but these are great big places where people live on top of one another and ride inside of tubes.

Town in Shetland is not like that. Tourists call it *Lerwick*, but it is more properly called *town* because it is the only one here. There are shops and garages and restaurants—all the things that are out in the country, just more of them gathered together in one place. Yet you only really need one of each.

There is a museum too, about how things were in the old days, nearly all the way back to the time of those who came before. The museum has a funny little room called a *trowie knowe*, which apparently resembles the abodes of things inside the hills. They have even created a pig of the old Shetland type, with bristles and everything, to show what they were like. The museum is very realistic, much of it, though it must be said that when these things really did happen, they did not happen inside of glass cases accompanied by explanatory signage. How it is they can understand more about the past now than they did when the past was actually happening, I do not know. It is a gift they have, this way of making everything simple. They make words for things that do not exist and create whole stories about them so you feel you are really there. When looking at the museum displays, I sometimes forget I really was there, for there is much I do not recall having happened.

And yet. There are many words that are not, so many things that are for which they have not created words. It is as if they were from another world, and only very occasionally am I unable to distinguish the one world from the other. We walk the same grasses and touch the same walls, yet when I see through their dream eyes, it is all foreign and unreal.

The young man went to town. He took the bicycle to Walls, then continued by bus. First he went to the stationers on Commercial Street and bought some more pens and notebooks. Next he had a lunch consisting of a hot sandwich at the Peerie Shop Cafe, along with a big frothy coffee of some kind. Then he went to the archives, which are held at the museum, and looked at all these old papers relating to Paul Stevens, who is dead but whose words they still keep. Which is a funny thing in itself.

By the time he was done, it was beginning to be late, and I wondered how he planned to get home after the last bus had run. But he had taken a room at the Grand, it seems, and was actually all prepared, with toothbrush and change of clothes and everything in his rucksack. And so he showered and thought of Sal, I guess, with the water running down.

I Have Not Answered

Though it was hard to tell for all the steam in the room.

After the shower, he wiped the condensation from the mirror and scrutinised his nakedness, squeezing his shoulders and patting his stomach. I noticed he had lost some weight since he first arrived. All of that bicycling maybe. And the fresh country air, people say.

He smiled at himself, but the smile turned bitter in his mouth, and he spat it out. He sat down naked upon the carpet in the main room, crossed his legs, and put his knuckles together. I was glad he did not have his smoke cones with him, the fumes of which produce in me a certain unease.

In a few minutes, he was dressed and out the door. His clothes were not particularly practical, though the season had not yet turned in earnest, and the evening rain was light. After a meal at Monty's, he crossed over Mounthooly Street and joined the smokers outside the Lounge. The sky was a dark blue, streetlights notwithstanding, and wind coursed the lane as he struggled to keep a flame up. A thickset Scottish sailor cupped his hands around the lighter, and the next instant, the cigarette tip was glowing. I have occasionally seen the young man smoke in the company of smokers. He apes their actions for ends best known to himself. A couple of Norwegians were joking by the wall, and a somewhat decrepit local was boasting to a pair of girls how he had joined the Masons thirty years since for the cheap beer. The young man said nothing. When he was done, he dropped the cigarette butt in a little metal box on the wall and entered the downstairs bar.

A casual game of darts was underway. The young man seated himself at the bar and chatted with the old ones, as is his wont. But this evening, he seemed restless.

The sounds of the session reached the bar from above, and the young man ascended to the lounge proper. A bunch of schoolgirls were playing the fiddle, and men of various ages were occupied on the guitar, accordion, and piano.

In music, they can join one another in ways they cannot in speech. There is a certain intimacy. It is perhaps because the sounds come from the instruments, not the players, so their own wills remain a step removed from the message in the tune. There is less danger that way, maybe, less exposure.

The young man drank intently, beer and whisky. Sometimes he spoke with people. Other times, he stared at nothing, or perhaps at the quiz machine, which is as good as nothing, and I got flickers of pictures in my eyes, quite unexpectedly.

A black-haired girl holding a harp and a chalice of wine.

But I checked, and the young man was not asleep, was not dreaming.

He fairly stumbled the short distance back to the Grand. The cobblestones glistened slick under the streetlights as rain slashed down. It chilled me. I felt feverish, ill.

The hotel room was still cold and damp from the young man's shower earlier in the evening. He grimaced, then returned himself to the carpet and sat again in silence.

But this time, it did not work. Instead of being at rest, his face was scrunched up, as though he were forcing his eyes shut, his mouth twisted in self-mockery. After a minute, he stood, his eyes now open but the cruel smile still on his face.

I shivered, the chill still with me though we had moved indoors.

He put his shoes back on and descended to the ground floor of the hotel. Though it was quite late by this point, festivities were still taking place in a room of the hotel named Posers, which is what they call a *nightclub*. I had never been to a nightclub before. It is like a very loud dance at the public hall in Walls, only with dearer drinks.

The music on the loudspeakers was of a sort with which I was unfamiliar. Though the music emanated from machines, and though the creators of the music – down in Aberdeen or somewhere – had used computers to make the sounds, I felt a vague organic presence behind it, some monotonous mad playing of pipes, or else the songs of whales in the night.

This nightclub, it was like an age before speech, before words.

Even I am not so old as that.

No one spoke. They made signs with their hands and faces, and sometimes they screamed—not for agony or for joy, nor even because the screams contained words for comprehending, but simply to be heard in their animal nature.

But I would not really know.

Was this a reverberation, clattering through the epochs, of the time of those who came before? Is this how it was?

At first, the young man just stood there amidst the madness, eyes glancing, that twisted smile contorting his face into something inhuman. Not inhuman as an animal, but as a god.

My head throbbed with the strangeness of it.

And then the young man was dancing madly, like one of those things that gather around the old stones and mounds and springs and holy places on the Nights of Crying.

I shuddered at the sight of him, so inhuman and uncontained. I wished almost not to see him. He was as fearful as a reflection, as one of us.

But all the people were strange, rubbing up against one another, these young things from the birth of the world, aping the actions of men and women when they are alone.

Then there was one in particular on which the young man had set his eyes and hands, a healthy looking blonde thing, though somewhat short and weirdly tanned. Were it not for her Shetland nose, I would have thought she had come up on the North Boat. Her clothes were flimsy and impractical, not at all suited for working the croft.

I distracted myself by wondering what it was she actually did, this creature. Perhaps she stood behind the counter at one of the shops in town. Or worked with computers for the Council. There are many of these animals that do, you know. Some even work with computers behind counters at shops. I am not at all sure what they do with these computers. But now, people have started carrying little computers around with them – which they nevertheless call *phones* – even at night. So whatever it is they do, it must be very important.

Yet my ponderings were futile too, for my attention was soon drawn back to the fearsome scene before me.

He was touching her breasts now, through the thin fabric of her blouse, having reached around from behind and sculpted himself against her contours. At one point, she rose from her delirium, noticed what he was doing, and pawed his hands away. But then she sank back into that mindless place, and his hands were there again, and she did not stop it.

My body buzzed, drawn toward oblivion by some strange attraction, utterly new to me. There was a fog through which I could not penetrate but past which an ancient song was calling.

It was hideous. I felt like screaming.

Which, you should know, is not a thing I ever do.

If it had been in my power, I would have crumbled them all to crumbs, every one of those animals. And I would have made a fire to perish them so that even the crumbs turned to ash. And I would have blown the winds out from the east, through the doors of the Grand, and into the nightclub, so that all the dust was blown away, out and away to Foula, where they would be damned forever, all in bits.

All except for him. He is different.

And then it occurred to me, of course, what he was doing. He was ever like one of those chameleons or mirrors or whatever. He was, of course, studying this girl. And when I pondered upon it, I realised that I had, in fact, heard rumours of activity of this kind at that place in South called Uni, where he comes from. Where they learn things. He might as well have had his recording machine with him, that is how much he was researching her. Oh, yes, I had been blind to it. I had forgotten how special this one is. He is not like all the others.

And even later, in the hotel room, as they hurried to undress one another upon the bed, he refused to kiss her, and I thought how very like him this was. I imagined him writing his fieldnotes: *With full awareness of the reflexive nature of ethnography, I nonetheless refrained from creating a situation of such intimacy as is unconducive to scientific inquiry*. And then too when he guided her onto her knees and pushed her head down onto the pillow, so as not – it seemed to me – to see her face, thus acquiring the appropriate scientific distance. His scholarly devotion was extraordinary, not like those others, who act, unwilled, for the pleasure or the pain of it.

He appeared to move instinctively, as through a blind attraction of points.

But I knew otherwise. There is a monumental plan behind all he does, for he is a manifestation of will. He is the law, the closing of the circle. With his will, he could do anything.

As he writhed against her, she lifted her head and groaned. His eyes blinked at the blondeness. He hesitated in his movement, seemed afraid.

This angered me. Why should she cause him to doubt his research? There was nothing fearful in her. She was an animal, a loathsome creature, and deserved to be destroyed utterly.

I Have Not Answered

That is what I would have done, had it been in my power.

And then he changed again, his face flashing furious and black. He withdrew his right hand and brought his palm swiftly down upon her, eliciting a sharp gasp. He started at the sound, frowned darkly, and hit her, approaching a punch.

I felt the need to shut my eyes against all the will he had.

And when he was done, he slid off her and onto the bed beside her. She slumped with a groan onto her stomach, then rolled over onto her side.

Without ever having spoken a word to one another, they fell asleep.

★

It was a sleep of alcohol, monstrous, deep beyond even dreams. It was already morning when a dream at last filled my eyes. A blonde woman was holding a paper bag, and he was placing bottles of wine in it, one by one. A white wine, then a red. I saw the bottles reflected in her eyes. Then his hand held a knife, and into her heart he plunged it, her blue woollen jumper sodden dark. She fell to the floor of the shop.

He woke with a jolt.

A funny dream, that.

His eyes were open wide.

He closed his eyes, scrunching them shut. Softly, so softly I had to strain to hear, he said to himself, "Shukongojin, Bosatsu of Determination, teach me control over my passions.

I dedicate myself to enlightenment and the liberation of all living things." He lay silent for the space of perhaps two minutes, perfectly motionless save for a slight trembling of the eyelashes.

And when he opened his eyes again, he found himself still staring at the girl's naked, weirdly bronzed back, lit by the faint light coming through the brown curtains.

With great stillness, he positioned himself and plunged into her. She woke immediately, of course, but by the time she had gained full presence, it was over.

He got out of bed and made straight for the bathroom, not even pausing as he took up his rucksack on the way. I was of two minds whether to follow him, but as my head was throbbing, I stayed where I was for the ease of it. The girl was sitting now, knees tight against her chest and the sheets pulled up around her. She was staring through me, at the black TV screen, and did not react when the shower came on in the other room. After a while, she began running her fingers through her tangled hair and smoothing it back over her shoulders.

When he came out of the bathroom, he was fully dressed. Seating himself in the chair by the window, he looked at her.

She seemed uncomfortable under his gaze. "You're a tourist? Here on business?"

He said nothing.

"That's good," she said, meeting his eyes. "That's good."

"Is it so different with Shetland men?"

I Have Not Answered

"No different."

"I'm not sure that's a compliment."

"The difference is, I never have to see you again. We won't meet on the Street or in a café."

"Ah. But we'll always know one another, in some sense."

"In twenty years' time, you'll never be my future husband's best friend. You'll never wonder whether to say anything, and I'll never wonder whether you've said it. I'll never be making tea, with you sitting at the table in the open kitchen and me having to wonder whether you're thinking about how you fucked me in 2014."

The young man said nothing.

"Safe sex," she said.

"My name's Innes."

"OK."

"I'm staying out in the Westside for a while. We could get together again sometime."

She glanced at the table clock. "Check-out is at 10:00."

★

I HOPE YOU'RE WELL, he wrote. *I was in Lerwick doing archival work yesterday. Afterward I went to the Lounge Bar and heard some tunes. It's the place for music in Shetland. You would've liked it. I'm thinking about you all the time.*

He put down the pen, laying it alongside some bits of driftwood and tufts of wool in the corner of the writing table.

There were tears in eyes. He poured himself a full glass of whisky in the kitchen and gulped it down. He never drinks when at the cottage, so I had been surprised when he had bought the bottle that morning.

He lit a cigarette and drew upon it deeply. Which is odd since he never smokes when he is alone.

But I don't know. Sometimes life's really strange and I wonder what I'm doing here. I feel alienated like I'm standing back watching myself going through the motions and doing what I do. You always said the best thing about me is that I care. I think I care. Or maybe I just pretend to care because I'm really someone else who's not like that at all. Maybe I'm just a mirror if that makes any sense.

I don't know what I'm reflecting.

The young man crumpled the paper into a ball and left it lying on the table. Another glass of whisky, another cigarette, and he went to bed. He tried thinking of Sal but seemed distracted by something and gave up.

I waited that night, sitting quite idly in the corner of the room. Time passed indeterminately, for he was not dreaming, and I did not feel like reading. I just sat there, thoughtless.

Or rather, almost thoughtless, for I thought about a mirror that does not know what it reflects, and I wondered what it would be like to see through the eyes of such a mirror. And imagined I saw in this mirror something like a sort of doll – a grotesque, crudely hewn plaything – lying slack in the dark corner of the room, its limbs limp and unmanipulated, its eyes lifeless and dull. Its smile dead. And I thought to myself that if I could see this thing in the mirror, then I must be the doll. And then, I thought, there would be no way of knowing, really, whether I were actually looking at a mirror facing my corner of the room or whether I were, in fact, looking at another doll in another corner, in which case I would not know whether I myself were a mirror or a doll either—except that, if we both were mirrors, there would have to be a doll somewhere or other, else we would have nothing to reflect. And if that were so, this doll would need to have faces and arms and legs and dull eyes and dead smiles on each side, on every side, circling endlessly, eternal in its repetition. The horror of this thought was so splendid, so acute, I shivered, felt the chill of an uncanny presence, which echoed back at me, chuntered into my cold bones from all the dark corners of the world. Exposed to the distilled evil of this presence, its sheer malignance, all pervasive, all around me, inhabiting my own skin, I sensed I was very near to perishing at the reflection of it.

Then, just in time, it occurred to me that I could not be seeing through the eyes of a mirror, for mirrors do not have eyes. And thus was the spell broken, and the presence receded so utterly fast and complete that one could have sworn the young man and I were alone in the room, always had been, always would be, unchanging, like dolls in a doll house.

Thoughtless and calm once more, I drifted toward slumber.

The young man woke with a jolt, and I too became alert.

There was fog at the window, impenetrable.

I could not tell if it were night or morning.

Slowly, he pulled off the sheets and stood. He walked over to the window in his nakedness and peered out. The cold travelled through the glass and bored into his nipples, which hardened at its touch.

"I trusted you."

I looked around the room, but we were alone.

He turned away from the window, and there were tears in his eyes.

"I trusted you."

Part II

THE TURNING OF THE SEASONS is a subtle thing, for a vengeful wind can blow from the west any time at all. It less surprising in the Westside, a land of sky watchers. Yet even here, an early summer hail may catch them off-guard, and they will scurry after shelter wherever it may be found. The salted rains too sweep in from the Atlantic whenever they please. There is no accounting for weather, which is a thing that is very old.

Weather has occasioned many a fight and tryst. Here in the country, shelter is rare, with perhaps a single overhanging ledge, lee of a hill, or ruined croft house in a whole wide expanse. But if you seek shelter, you must be prepared to meet anything there. Friend or enemy or crawling thing or neighbour's wife. This is, indeed, how the Walls line of Millars came to be. The others could merely guess at how the Neely cheekbones had entered the Millar bloodline. But I did not have to guess. I was there when it happened, in the half-collapsed byre at the head of Lera Voe, overlooking Vaila.

The crawling things whisper that Vaila is the Isle of the Fertile Dew, a place of which such wild tales have been told for so very long that they must be either entirely true or not at all. And perhaps there is something in it then, if the Walls line of Millars was conceived in Valia's shadow. But I have some doubts on this point, for there are now but two people living on Vaila, where there once were many. It is said as well that cats avoid the place, choosing rather to attempt the swim across Wester Sound than remain on the island if brought. But what this might have to do with the Isle of Fertile Dew eludes me. Anyway. I would not go there, just in case.

It is a funny thing that May Stevens did not return to Uni at summer's end. The turning of the seasons was perhaps too subtle, and she missed it. It might be that you must be there at the start if you want to participate, like betting on a cock fight. But I would not really know either way. I have never looked it up on the internet. I think I shall, one day, perhaps.

This Uni place, it is a place spread out over all the world, in Aberdeen, in Glasgow, in London, and even in America and the land of the Chinese people who make the plastic toys they sell at Harry's in town. That a place can be so vast is truly something. It must be all in bits.

I should like to visit, maybe, but I do not know. If I did, I would steal an Ordnance Survey map first so I knew all the exotic place names and could roll them around in my mouth like the hard coloured candy they had in a jar at the old shop in Aith. And I would go there to Uni, and they would see me, for once I knew the names, I would not need to fear them.

Uni must, at any rate, be quite different from Shetland. In the autumn, it is often dark here, and there is a strange thing about the light then. Early in the afternoon, at an uncertain hour, the light seeps to the west, forming a dread halo behind Foula. For a space of some minutes, the island is all black and terrible, revealed as the dead hellish place it is.

You would not want to see it, I assure you. But perhaps, there would be no harm in it, seeing Foula at that uncertain time, before it has set its mask in place, all peaceful and lovely.

Then you would know it as I do.

In my walks across the moors, I have sometimes heard mutterings, low and indistinct, that Foula is not to blame. "It is a creature of its nature," they say, "and there are kernels of us that we cannot alter. Does not the blame lie, rather, with those who came before, in whose image were sculpted all the great atrocities of this world? Is it not they who bade the Earthy Things build for them great temples of rock and stone and peat, that people should one day raise little houses upon these temples and put miniature sheep there and live out their births and lives and deaths there, all so that these monstrous stone altars might be soaked through with consecrating blood?"

But no, I say, those who came before are beyond blame. They simply are.

"Does not the blame lie, then, with the Earthy Things, who chose, unbidden, to satiate the slumber urges of the great expanses sleeping in the deep earth? Would not those who came before have otherwise withered and died up? Are not they to blame, the Earthy Things? There sits Foula, a slave to its own nature. Show it pity, that it might be saved. Yes, make offering to it, and consecrate its stone with blood, that it might be awakened from its damnation, for which it is not to blame. See that man there? That man casting peat? If you took it now, there would be none who remembered it in five thousand years. That man, it is like the bubble in the burn, which passes and breaks, unmissed. There is a blade in the rocks. You know where. Carve this man up and spill its blood on Foula, as a rebuke to the Earthy Things, who sculpted all the evil in the world."

These voices have no power over me.

I have been called, but I have not answered.

They just mutter on the moors, impotent through the epochs. Whether they were insane from the beginning or whether it is their impotent muttering that has made them so, I do not know.

And it occurs to me, this, because of the young man's story. When he is out speaking with the old folk, he hears all kinds of stories about trows, many of which I myself have never heard. Although he never tells them what tale he is seeking, I have, over time, come to recognise his hints and prods in its direction, so that I perhaps have a fair idea of it.

It is an old story, if I am right, and I believe it must be quite true, though not in Shetland. I would have known

I HAVE NOT ANSWERED

about it had it happened here. But word spreads from parts, I suppose, for it really is quite horrific the way they went about it. There are kernels of our nature we cannot alter, but it is dangerous to go as far as that. There was no need to destroy her so entirely. It is possible to take the body yet to let the soul remain within. As a rule, they are weak creatures, and much can be achieved through manipulation of the passions. There is no need to destroy them utterly.

But anyway. I have no interest in that anymore. I cannot even recall whether I once did. So much has changed, though we remain, and memories coalesce over the epochs, clattering backward.

But I am sure I never did that.

Their bodies, maybe, but never that.

★

THE BEACH WAS COLD but the day bright. In his hand, the young man held a bit of driftwood. It had been smoothed by the waves, which cast themselves upon the sands as doomed whales seeking death, never accomplished. Death, in its finality, is beyond even the sea.

In the bit of driftwood, there was a hole where a nail once had been. The young man held the wood up to his eye and looked through the hole. The great wide ocean was before him, and I suppose that, through the hole, it looked no less wide. He held in his other hand a tuft of wool he had collected from the fence at Finnigarth. This tuft of wool, he lifted it into the air and released it. It began to fall, then the wind picked it up and carried it off over the water toward Foula. Something about this made my head throb, but I cannot say what, for there is no danger in it. Wool is an inert animal thing, of no harm to anyone.

The young man sat down on the shingle. The day was cold, but he was practically dressed. He held a notebook in his lap and wrote in his cramped little scientific lettering. *11 October. No success yet with search. Trip to Burravoe provided no new evidence re: 'King Orfeo'.*

A change came over his face, which quivered into abstraction. When he resumed writing, it was in the kind of lettering he had used when writing to Sal, back when he still answered her letters and before he removed the battery from his mobile phone.

You can't speak with Graham. Sometimes you wonder if he's really there and you have the urge to find someplace hidden so you can watch where he lives and lie in wait for him. What would you even say if you could speak with him? You'd maybe tell him you've loved him all this time. That he isn't as useless as he thinks.

His life has a purpose and it is you. You're here for him. You can give meaning to the last thing of value he has left. He must give it to you before it's too late. Without it, everything's meaningless. All this for nothing, and the cycle must continue. But he's obstinate in his animal nature and doesn't realise. For him it is useless. You could build from it something great. It weighs him down, drags him toward rebirth. If you could take it from him he could die peacefully and his name would be remembered forever clattering through the epochs.

My memory is not what it once was. Or rather, I cannot remember what my memories once were. Things are not the same. But maybe they are, and I simply cannot recollect if it is so. Yet everything echoes backward. The other day, I found myself wondering when the Northmen would come and destroy the Pictish tribes. For a moment, I had thought it was still long ago, like I was inside one of those glass cases at the museum. But men are just a small piece of the past, a little bit of it. They only appear more real than the other bits because they are more recent.

Maybe he doesn't even know your name. He doesn't know you're here for him. If he did he'd supplicate himself at your feet and give himself to you utterly. You'd carve out the story from him and his name would live forever, a contribution to the liberation of all living things. But he thinks the story belongs to him. It doesn't. It belongs to everyone. It belongs to you because only you have the power to understand it and to pass on its message. Once you have it you'll share it with the world. Most will ignore it and will continue their dull animal lives as if asleep. But some will understand it and your name will live forever. And you will have come a step closer to awakening. You will

The young man's face quivered back to its previous state. He stopped writing. Holding the pen before his eyes, he looked at it as if it were a foreign thing, blinking a few times. Then he looked down at the paper, read what he had written, and tore the sheet from the notebook in disgust. He crumpled it up, lifted it to the wind, and released it.

Are men a piece of the future too? Sometimes I ponder upon it. As far as I recollect, I always used to think that they were not or that they were but a very small bit of it at most.

But this one is different, and I wonder if he is a new sort of man and if a new epoch is coming. All ages are more or less the same, except for the age before everything, when everything was different. So the new age will probably be the same too, only in a different way.

For all I know.

★

THERE WAS A PARTY at the Stevens' house to celebrate May's twenty-second birthday, and those of her friends who were not yet living in South were there. They had come all the way up from town just for the occasion. Laurie had bought her a gold chain as a present. It really was very shiny and pretty. I was reminded of the sun on a string of lochs, a strand of shining black hair, the string of a harp.

There were bottles of wine and cans of beer and all sorts of spirits. What they did not finish that night, Graham would manage for them soon enough.

Where Graham was, I do not know, but I was not surprised by his absence. Maybe he was at Hermaneuk Inn or perhaps Ron Seatton's at Vesquoy.

I Have Not Answered

The young man spoke with May's friends. He was quick with his answers and made jokes and everything. He is quite good at talking about things that have no meaning. Every so often, he looked over to May and Laurie. That is only logical, for of all the people at the party, he knows them best.

Eventually, various instruments were brought forth that they might sing and play. Laurie played a country thing on his guitar, and there were others who joined in with fiddle and banjo. And so it went, with everyone taking turns to lead. When it was the young man's turn, he pretended not to notice. But he could not escape it, for with them, the round of music is a sacred thing, a circle that must not be broken.

Laurie asked, "Do you play?"

The young man feigned surprise. "Oh, no. Not really."

"Does du no play the fiddle?" asked May. "Give wis a tune."

Despite his protestations, a fiddle was placed in the young man's hands. His fingers trembled. "Actually..."

"Du's no embarrassed of wis!" May began laughing.

"Actually, I feel rather like the guitar."

Laurie passed him his own, and the young man looked it over. He struck a single, harsh note and held the guitar uneasily, as if unsure of its nature. But I have heard him on the fiddle, and he is proficient enough at that.

The young man looked at May, then inclined his chin so he stared at the wall above her head. A voice rose from his throat, so passionate, strange, and foreign that he seemed possessed by the spirit of another. It was not as I had heard him sing before. I glanced around but sensed no uncanny presence in the room.

In Scarlet Town where I was born,
There was a young man dwelling.
He courted a pretty fair maid,
Whose name was Barbara Allen,
    Whose name was Barbara Allen.

His playing was clumsy, his voice strange, and the room was very quiet. Laurie looked away. May faltered slightly, then joined on the refrain.

He courted her for seven years,
Till he could court no longer.
Till he fell sick and very ill,
And sent for Barbara Allen,
    And sent for Barbara Allen.

It's slowly she put on her clothes,
And slowly she came walking,
And when she came to his bedside
'Young man,' she says, 'you're dying,'
    'Young man,' she says, 'you're dying.'

'Oh, dying I cannot be,
One kiss from you would cure me.'

I Have Not Answered

'One kiss from me you shall not get
Though your poor heart lies breaking,
Though your poor heart lies breaking.'

There was a moistness in the young man's eyes, but he could not have been crying, for he stared so pointedly at that spot on the wall, and there was nothing there to make him cry.

She had not been a mile from town,
Before she heard the death bells tolling.
And every toll they seemed to say,
'Cruel-hearted Barbara Allen,
Cruel-hearted Barbara Allen.'

The young man broke off unexpectedly, before the tale reached its close. The others clapped, grunted encouragingly, and did those things they do to show appreciation whether or not they mean it.

The round of music turned to the next celebrant, who played a cheery Shetland tune called 'Da Farder Ben da Welcomer'.

But there was a certain tension that I could not explain. They are odd, the way they think.

Laurie poured himself a large rum and drank it quickly. An instant later, the young man did the same.

★

The storm was dying, yet the air was still loud from the west, forcing the ebb tide far up the beach. The young man looked out to Foula, a bastion of peace in violent waters.

If only he could have seen the Kame then, waves smashing against the cliffs and being pummelled to spray. Against such mad resilience, it is the ocean that is to be pitied.

He stood where the grass dropped away at the edge of the beach, and such was the noise of the air that he heard nothing. It was only when he came farther down that he saw the two figures at the other end of the shingle. Both man and beast were silent, but I could tell the young man marked something uncanny in the scene. I felt it too, though differently, for my senses are keener than theirs.

The young man walked toward them. I think he realised from how it lay that the grey seal was dead. Graham Stevens did not look up until the very last, but he seemed unsurprised. I guess he had seen the young man coming down off the turf. Sea foam skittered across the shingle, congregating windward of the seal's corpse.

"Washed up in the storm," Graham said when the young man was close enough to hear. "Been dead some days."

The young man looked from Graham to the seal and back again. Then he glanced around the beach as if he expected someone to be watching.

"I come here most days," the young man said. "I've never seen you."

"No."

I Have Not Answered

"It's a pretty spot."

"Grew up on this beach. Don't need to visit. Tourists. Nothing special to me."

"Still nice to come back every so often?"

"There's things wash up after a storm. Some of them, a man can use. Yun house du's biding in. Was a time she was roofed with rafters that came ashore here. Werena rafters then, mind. But one finds uses."

"Where did they come from?"

"Dunna ken. Ship of some kind. Find all sorts on the beach. Nuts from South America even. If du's lucky."

The young man nodded toward the seal. "And that?"

"In the old days maybe. Nought it's good for now. Too far gone. Skinned it before the rot set in, and du could've had dysel a nice waistcoat. Like as when we hunted them."

"Did you...?"

"No, boy. Before my time. Grandfather's, maybe. Great-grandfather's. A man wouldna hunt seals if he could help it. And things got so as a man could help it. More money. Clothes and things brought up on the North Boat. Gore-Tex lining. No, sealing's had its day." Graham bent down and laid his hand on the corpse. "Not a bit of heat left in her. Doesna take long. But I wonder. If du had the instruments – thermometers so sensitive – whether du couldna measure just the smallest bit of heat left behind. Everything that's ever been alive must have a touch of heat in it, ken? Even rock that once was deep and hot in the earth. There'd be a bit of heat left. After all this time. With the right instruments?"

"I'm not sure."

"Something tells me, 'Go to the beach today, Graham Stevens.' A little voice inside my head. Du kens. Intuition."

"They say it's strongest in women."

"Well, I dunna ken. Maybe that's the truth. There's no women, at any rate, come out here to find nought but a dead selkie. Could just be masculine intuition's usually wrong."

Graham took a flask from his pocket and drank. He offered it to the young man, who did not cringe at the bad whisky.

The wind had slowed considerably, and a stench of death came up from the seal. It still had one eye. It is said that eyes are glassy after death, but that depends on what kind of glass and how long after death you see them. This eye was like a round of frosted glass brought up on the North Boat. The animal was bloated, but decay had been delayed by the cold. I do not know where the corpse had lain before washing ashore here. Had it been in the water all this time, the fish would have taken more of it, but had it been on land, the birds would surely have got the second eye.

Graham gestured toward the animal. "Kenned this selkie since she was a bairn. Oh, aye. One gets to know them by sight. Placement of the eyes, pattern on the head. She was born on Sel Ayre, bit north. Been swimming these waters all this time. Twenty years, give or take."

"How did it die?"

"Dunna ken. Sometimes they just die. No reason. Mind, there's them that are shot. But this one? No, she's just dead."

They stood looking at the seal.

"Say they're evolved from bears. Du wouldna think it."

"I've heard a lot of things said about them. Folks say that, in the old days, it was thought they could turn into people."

"Ach, no. There's folk say all kinds of rubbish. No saying there werena tales. But that's no the same as believing, ken? Du shouldna come away thinking we're all savages, believing in trows and such. No matter what John's been telling dee." Graham wiped his mouth on his sleeve. "Well, du kens. Wis that growed up before the oil think different on things. It's no good dwelling on the past. My daughter, sometimes I'm thinking she's more Shetland than me. Me and Margaret, we're just folk from Shetland. But May's *a Shetlander*. That's who she is, ken? Same with her man, Laurie."

The young man stared at the seal.

"They *feel* a way about it. My generation, we just live it. There's exceptions, mind. Folk that write articles and work in museums. Du's been speaking with them, I doubt. But I'm no certain they're more Shetland than the rest of wis."

"I'm proud of my own place," the young man said.

"That's the way of it, ken? We each of wis has wir own place, and as I see it, that's fine. Aberdeenshire, London, Shetland. Sure, they're all fine."

★

I ONCE READ something somewhere by a minister called Robert Kirk, who lived in South many years since. It must have been long ago I read it, if ever I read it at all and it is not just a thing I imagine. Yet the words remain with me: *They do not all the harm which appearingly they have power to do; nor are they perceived to be in great pain, save that they are usually silent and sullen. They are said to have many pleasant toyish books; but the operation of these pieces only appears in some paroxysms of antic corybantic jollity, as if ravished and prompted by a new spirit entering into them at that instant, lighter and merrier than their own. Some say their continual sadness is because of their pendulous state, as uncertain what at the last revolution will become of them, when they are locked up into one unchangeable condition; and if they have any frolic fits of mirth, 'tis as the constrained grinning of a mort-head, or rather as acted on a stage, and moved by another.*

Whenever I recollect on this, I think of the things in Deepdale. They wish to cross over to the other side but cannot when the burn is flowing. Yet when it is frozen, they move back and forth as if compelled. Perhaps a spirit has entered into them, and they would not be so horrible if they could get free of it. A spirit is to blame for the things they do. I have seen them, with my own eyes, take a body and do such things to it that its soul fled away, and only bloody tatters remained. There was a wife called Kerry who died this way. The people, in their ignorance, waked her remains nine nights through to drive the spirits from them. This was, however, just superstition, for there was nothing left by that point.

I Have Not Answered

But that was long since, I assure you. I do not believe the things in Deepdale know about the Council or have any conception of the world in progress outside the valley. There is, perhaps, an instinct that restrains them from doing all the harm they have power to do. For if the police went there, and the health inspectors, and eventually ministers and hippie spiritualists and Japanese people with swords, I do not know what would become of them. Maybe they would learn to read books and become policemen and health inspectors or otherwise work with computers. But I cannot really say. Theirs is a small world.

I was thinking this as the young man slept. It was dark in the room, but my eyes had adjusted, so I could see almost as well as in the simmer dim.

But then it got darker again, and it took me a moment to realise he was dreaming. There was very nearly nothing to see, just the ghosts of uneven contours, resembling walls. A smell was there, like a thing rotting in the dark, and the millennial reek of ancient earth.

As his dream eyes adjusted to the dark, the vision grew clearer. He was in a tunnel, the walls low and narrow, slopped with mud. He did not look back but moved forward, and there was something like light far ahead. Very like light. It was, I thought, something like the putrid phosphorescence that rises from dead rotting whales that have thrown themselves upon the shore and die at last, crushed under their own horrific weight. The mud sucked at his boots as he walked, and the ground was sick. Yet the walls changed with his progression, and the mud thinned, until at last the tunnel was of stone, smeared with phosphorescent fungal putrescence that lit dim the crudely hewn passage.

Yes, it was hewn, I am sure of it, carved perhaps into the Earth itself or else into a stone of such expanse as the mind cannot fathom. What mad effort must have been made to carve this tunnel, and by whom? I cannot say whether the young man asked himself this in his dream, but it is what I would have been asking if I were him. If I had the capacity to dream.

After miles of trekking through these dead corridors, an end appeared, a little alcove of sorts in which a figure sat.

I had thought before the tunnel walls were black, but this was not the case, for compared with this figure, the stone was white as chalk. Its skin was black, and its eyes were so black I could not at all perceive them, and through the gaps in its cap of beads sprouted hair in white tufts, like bits of wool that one may find stuck to the fence at Finnigarth. Its black knuckles were joined atop its crossed legs, with the soles of its feet pointing up. It was a little man, perfect in all respects yet distorted into perfection's opposite, as seen through a backlit pane of frosted glass. Its countenance was soft and fine, friendly even, and its limbs were flawless in proportion. Yet it appeared through this distortion – for distortion it must have been – a hideous malformation, the afterbirth that follows the futile contractions of the Earth.

I Have Not Answered

Although it did not move, I sensed it lived.

The young man approached, unhesitant, incautious, and I saw it held in its hands a thing very like a jagged bit of black stone. The young man crouched so as better to see. And this was a queer thing, for when I looked closely, I saw the stone was not entirely black at all but was topped with a thin veneer of green, and there were little croft houses on it and miniature sheep roaming the slopes, and tiny little people, ever so small, dying and living and being born all on this bit of rock.

The young man entered a croft house. Inside, all was in disarray, as if the skeletons siting around the upturned table had jumbled all the furnishings before they died. And in the hearth sat a little man, white as chalk, its eyes closed as if in sleep. It was a hideous malformation yet through some strange distortion – as the dribble of blood that follows the ineluctable death pangs of the Earth – appeared perfect in all respects.

And in its hands, it held a polished globe of opal. And on this globe of opal, there was a thing very like a sea, writhing with the bloated songs of rotting whales.

The young man woke with a start.

A funny dream, that.

Going to the kitchen, he splashed water on his face from the faucet. He made coffee and drank it quick and shaking, its heat notwithstanding. He put on his clothes and went out.

The young man walked up to the cliffs and followed their curving declension to the north until he came to the beach. At the far end of the shingle, Graham Stevens stood alongside the grey seal corpse. The young man came to them. Both the seal's eyes were missing, and its rot hung in the night.

Graham drew out his flask. He took a swig and handed it to the young man, who drank of it. They stood there, staring at the seal, smoking and drinking, until the time when it would have been dawn were the Earth not already well into its long pull toward winter.

And with the coming of the dawn that did not come, they returned wordlessly to their homes.

★

I'M ALWAYS THINKING of you, he wrote on a sheet of paper. *I'm always seeing your eyes before me and smelling your scent beside me. Rain and peat and sheep and the salt wind. You will think I do not know what I'm thinking but the words you say fill me with hope for something infinite. You are part of the land which is part of you. To you the tides make homage twice a day. Everything belongs to a universal logic, has its own proper and beautiful place. My place is beside you. I've achieved the perspective to see that now. I used to think I loved someone else but now I know that was different. Back then I didn't know what love is.*

They think words can change things. But things will always be the same. At night in summer, there is a light called the *simmer dim*, which is disparate and strange, with flashes of darkness in between, as though filtered out in the far off, beyond our reach. And in winter, everything is reversed, so at midday there comes a disparate darkness flashed by bits of light. The one and the other are always present, and the cycle will never be complete. When you think it is on the cusp of completion, it all begins again.

I know a place where there are lights in the hill at night. At times, I have even seen them myself. They wink on and off, then are silent. You might imagine they are winking at you, but this would be a mistake. Their reason is known only to themselves, if even that. And if they *should* happen to wink at you, their reason would be no clearer. You would know only your reason, not theirs. By that same law, there dwell in the lochs calling things, which are best left unanswered. For their call is their own, though the answer is yours, and it is thus you come into their power. It does not happen through words, which are themselves without meaning. It happens through making the effort that words make manifest. It is safest to make no effort at all.

I've heard the whales sing for you far out at sea and seen the mareel lap the shore with bioluminescence in your honour. I lack words for you. There will never be enough. And it doesn't matter if you love another. This can only accentuate the purity of what I feel which is not for physical material things. That which grows from the mud can yet be pure. My love is like the endless song of a harp which repeats but is different every time. I came here for you. I've always loved you.

For a moment, I imagined he was writing to me. Even though I knew I imagined it, I was nevertheless filled with a feeling resembling that which they call *happiness*.

Which, you should know, is not a thing I ever feel.

He placed his pen on the writing table, looked down at the paper, read what he had written, sighed, and crumpled it up into a tight ball. Turning, he looked over at the little statue of the little man sitting on the reading table.

Yesterday, he had been in town. There was a queer thing happening, the likes of which I had not seen before. It was a thing called *yoga club*, where 23 people come together in a big bright room and try to twist their bodies into funny shapes. Some were better at it than others. I imitated them, to see what it was like, but it was no challenge at all, my nature being, perhaps, more malleable than theirs. Seeing them all there together, I realised for the first time that the young man must have practiced these things, these ways of sitting and moving, at some point in the past, before I had known him. Why anyone would wish to acquire such skills, I cannot say.

After the session, the young man took a cup of tea with the instructor, a middle-aged woman from South. At first, they just spoke of technical things, how to sit and that, so I got bored and stopped listening. Then I realised they had moved on to another topic.

The woman said, "Anyone can be a bodhisattva. The vow, the striving toward Buddhahood, is what makes the difference."

The young man said, "Even the Buddha first had to travel the path of asceticism. It was only then he found the Middle Way. First he had to starve his passions."

"No. You overcome passions by setting your mind toward enlightenment, not by focusing on the passions."

"It's a matter of expediency," he said. "If your passions interfere with your ability to assist others, they must be destroyed. There's a chain of causality to it. This is the law. It's set forth in the sutras."

The woman smiled. "The law only becomes clear when you've awakened to your role within it."

The young man departed yoga club soon after. Before leaving town, he bought a bottle of expensive whisky from the supermarket. He seemed restless and dissatisfied on his trip back to the Westside, though he put on a pleasant face for the man from whom he hitched a ride to Weisdale.

The next day, once he was done crumpling up the letter he had written, he took the bottle of whisky out of the cupboard. He placed it in his rucksack and went out.

The beach was empty. But not entirely so, for the corpse of the grey seal still lay there. It stank of death, had provided a feast for numerous birds and crabs, I know not how many. The young man took his position not far from it. Not directly downwind, where the smell would have been unbearable for any length of time, but not wholly outside the aura of decay.

He stood there, as though waiting for something to happen.

Some time passed, then a sound came from farther up the beach. I realised I had been dozing there in the cold. Graham Stevens headed straight to the rotting thing, knelt down, and placed his hand on a patch of skin that was drier and more intact than the rest. He left his hand there a moment, as if feeling for life. Then he went over to the young man.

"Nice day for it," the young man said.

"Aye."

The young man took out the whisky, uncorked it, and took a gulp from the bottle. He handed it to Graham.

"Tell me," said the young man, "about selkies."

"There isna much to tell."

"What makes them special?"

"Ach, they're no so special as all that. Selkie's just an animal." Graham took two drinks, then handed the bottle back to the young man. For a while, he said nothing. "But I suppose it's to do with their eyes, ken? They've these great big dark eyes, and the way they look at a man, he'd think..."

"I hadn't noticed."

"No. Well. It's not always. But when they know dee. If du's on the shore or the boat, they'll swim over, stick their big long heads out the water, and take a good look at dee. They recognise folk, no question. What they think of wis... Well."

"This one hasn't eyes anymore."

"First things to go. Most nutritious part. But what those eyes saw in life, yeah? Whole world there underwater, with all its own forests and hills and even peerie houses for the fishes. Du has to wonder. Because they kens all about wir world too, ken? Can see it when they sticks their heads out and come ashore. But wis, we kens only the one place."

"Maybe our one place is enough."

"Well, du kens better than I."

"I'm not sure."

"Du's the expert doing the research."

"I just study stories."

"Ach, well. There's enough of them, at least."

The young man took another drink then made a little depression in the stones and set the bottle into it. He lit a cigarette in the shelter of the crest of the beach. It was cold, and the wind had picked up.

"There was a man," said Graham. "Name of Tom Grayson. Living in Sandness. Died of cancer, oh, ten years back. And before he passed, he says he'll come back and visit. Return to Sandness after he's gone, ken? Come and see his old friends."

"And did he?"

"That's no for me to say. But the day after he passed, there comes a big old selkie inta the harbour and hauls himself up onto the slipway at Ness of Melby. Bearded seal. They're no common in these parts. But they're no so uncommon either as to make dee think anything of it. But it was the timing. There was folk said it was Tom come back. And right enough, that selkie hung about a few weeks, on the slipway or in the bay. Then it went off again. Which is, mind, what a big old selkie like that would do if it found itself some hundreds of miles from home. No, boy. They're just animals. Been folk filling your head with stuff."

"But there was a time..."

"Well. Before my time."

"Your great-grandfather's time?"

"So long I canna tell dee what time it was."

"Tradition has it that if one of the seal people was injured by a hunter, its wound could only be healed by the hunter himself. And once a hunter heard the selkie folk's wails of mourning, he'd be moved by pity never to hunt again. The seal and the hunter, they were one another's redemption."

"Yeah. That's tradition," Graham said. He took a drink. "And du doesna believe it any more than me."

"But mightn't there be a kernel of truth in it? Truth of some kind?"

"Aye, aye, I hear dee. Sure, there's truth of some kind in everything. Stories are just a way of telling."

The sky was violet with early dusk.

Somewhere to the north, a curlew cried out. I loved the curlew for its grace in the waters and its stillness upon the moor. Its cry drifted past, fragrant of worms, shellfish, mud. The cry quivered, wavered—and was pulled out to sea, where it would either wash up against hulking black Foula or else be drawn into the depths.

The time, I thought, is now. It is now I must act.

I wished to call out, to warn the cry back from its senseless damnation, but my throat closed up around my desire, and all that escaped my lips was a strangled laugh.

Is impotence the curse of eternity? To live forever and fail in one's doings? So intimate is the causality, I do not know which came first. Eternity cannot not abide an empowered will that sculpts time in its image. So instead it is inhabited by slack-limbed dolls, oh-so-lifelike but powerless in all that matters.

I Have Not Answered

I hate the curlew for exposing me for what I am.
I wish the curlew were dead.

★

THIS MAY STEVENS is not one to whom I had paid much attention. She is like the others in body and spirit. The young man had, however, taken an interest, intent on researching her to get close to her father. He is very cunning and subtle.

But she is just an animal, and I am certain she realises nothing.

Her room at the Stevens' house has posters on the walls and books on the shelves. One poster has the words 'The Clash' on it and shows a man about to smash a guitar, but another has no words at all and shows a moustached, long-haired man in a beret. Most of the books are on Engineering, which I understand to be the study of how things work, whatever that means. It must be a very big study at any rate, for so many things work so differently.

There is a white lamp and a glass of water on the table beside May's bed. Her bedclothes are of a rich purple complexion, and she sleeps in full-length pyjamas, with the top two buttons of the shirt undone. Of her dreams, there is little to say, save that they are mundane. I should, perhaps, have been glad for their entertainment before this summer, but now I yearn to be at the young man's bed. Last night, May dreamed she was with Laurie at Osla's Cafe Bar in town, discussing a concert. They ate savoury pancakes and had milkshakes.

When May woke in the morning, she checked her e-mail first thing. She then selected some practical clothes, took her towel off the back of the chair, and went to the bathroom, where she peed and showered. She did not, as far as I could tell, think of Laurie while bathing.

After she had dried herself and dressed, she gave her short black hair a cursory comb and applied a cream of some sort to her face and hands. She then sprayed herself with a perfume fragrant of mixed spring blossoms, honey, and thyme. I do not mean to suggest that I could discern this precise composition myself, but it said so on the label. The perfume bottle was a small, inadequate thing constructed from opaque lilac glass. As I thought it might interest the young man and be of use to him, I resolved to return for the bottle later in the day.

For now, I followed May downstairs to the kitchen.

Margaret was at the table, going through some bills. "We need to talk about your plans."

"Ach, Ma. I can have a cup coffee first, surely?"

"Are you going back to Glasgow?"

"Maybe."

"What happened?"

"There's nothing's happened."

"Oh."

"Maybe," said May. "Maybe I need to travel some first. See a bit of the world. Go to New Zealand maybe."

I Have Not Answered

Margaret opened her mouth, but before she could say anything, May spoke again, "I'd pay for it myself. Get some work there."

"What happened?"

"We have family on North Island. Them that wrote wis."

"May."

"Uni will still be there when I get back. I'd no lose my credits frae being away a year or two."

Margaret put down her papers and walked out of the room. May sighed and sat at the table. She wrote a message of some kind on her phone, but her fingers worked so quick, I could not read it.

A few minutes later, she went out. The first thing she did was look up the ridge of Murnin Kame to see how the weather lay. Sheep bleated from across the field. She ignored them and followed the road east, toward the village. It was a Saturday, and Laurie would be home.

If she knew how much she was being researched, she would not want to leave Shetland.

She would supplicate herself at the young man's feet and give herself to him utterly. He is of a superior kind and not possessed of their animal nature.

Later that day, May and Laurie copulated on the sofa at Laurie's house. It was all sweat and smells and noises.

But I did not mind. It is in their nature.

★

8 NOVEMBER. Spoken with Graham Stevens on the beach on numerous occasions, trying to guide him into storytelling. With him drunkenness is a matter of degrees and I have not observed that alcohol has any particular impact on his reticence to talk. He often relates anecdotes but never tells stories as such. Were it not for his reputation one would never imagine he was a storyteller of any sort far less that his father was a great one. He is obsessed with a dead seal on the beach. He has a haunted look about him.

The young man yawned and closed the notebook. He went into the bathroom. As he reached for his toothbrush, he saw a little opaque lilac bottle sitting on the shelf beside it and hesitated an instant before proceeding to brush his teeth. But all the while, he kept staring at the bottle. He leaned over and spat the toothpaste into the sink. Then he closed his eyes for a good ten seconds, still leaning over.

He straightened his back and opened his eyes.

The bottle was still there.

Some of the colour left his face. His eyes searched the corners of the tiny bathroom in the mirror. That failing, he drew aside the shower curtain. Turning back to the mirror, he placed a thumb and index finger on the bottle and stroked it slowly, then took it into his hand. Removing the cap, he sniffed the nozzle.

"Sal?"

There was no answer.

"May?"

He was shaking.

I Have Not Answered

"I love you."

A pleasant feeling rose inside me.

He sniffed again, then sprayed a little mist of perfume into the air. Mixed blossoms, honey, and thyme.

"And as soon as the Buddha entered upon meditation, there fell a great rain of divine flowers."

Though he had just brushed his teeth, he had a large glass of whisky in the kitchen before going to bed.

Soon he was dreaming.

He was in a dark hallway. At first, I thought it might be the tunnel from the other dream, but it was not at all dark enough for that, and besides, the floor was carpeted.

He crept along, very slowly, until he came to a white door, which he opened with the utmost delicacy, and entered a room. A bed was visible, and despite the dimness of the surroundings, I knew it was covered with purple bedclothes. The room was filled with the scent of some strange perfume. From the soft breathing, you could tell someone was sleeping there.

A black-haired head rested on the pillow, its face turned away. He walked up to the bed and pulled back the blanket, revealing a female body dressed in full-length pyjamas, with the top two buttons of the shirt undone. He reached out and stroked the sleeper's shoulder.

Then he woke.

★

I HAVE KNOWN John Millar since his birth. He was reckless in youth, is now solid in age. It is an age at which people stop demanding of others in hope that others will stop demanding of them. John was pleased to have someone to listen.

The digital audio recorder worked away silently on the table. It took in and immortalised every sound.

The coffee was very hot, and the young man managed it with a loud slurp. That too would be recorded for posterity.

"It was often asked," said John, "whether they had souls. Some held them to be demons, angels that were with Satan in his war against God. But others said they were angels that wouldn't take sides when the war broke out. And so God thought them too bad for Heaven but too good for Hell. So they ended up in the middle. Ended up here on Earth, ken?"

"Where've you learned this?" the young man asked.

"Oh, books and things."

"It's not something people ever talked about?"

"They might've done. Not in my day. Not since they stopped believing."

The young man wrote in his notebook, *John is talking and I am writing. I write so that John may talk.*

John saw the young man writing something. He grew bold with his own importance. "There's a story."

"Yes?"

"Well." John coughed. "There's a minister up in Sandness. And it's said that all Shetland ever got from Scotland was dear meal and greedy ministers. But this man up in Sandness, he's

I Have Not Answered

of a different sort. He learns the language, and he's ready to help folk on the croft when it's needed. So he's respected, ken? And word gets around that he's something of a theologian on the side. There's not many ministers that were. But this minister, if a man wants to talk about things, religion and whatnot, well, he's blide to do it. Likes nothing better. Pour you a glass of whisky and talk about God and angels and that."

"No wonder he was popular, what with the whisky."

"Aye, it's not a few men have turned to religion on account of drink. But so word gets around. And how they found out about it, I dunna ken, but there's one day this minister's sitting in the but-end, and in troops a whole flock of trows. They're wanting to speak with him, ken? And this minister is, I doubt, more than a peerie bit frightened, for trows are aye dangerous folk, no matter God's on your side.

"Well, this minister, he asks what they've come for. And one of these trows, he pipes up and says, 'We'll hear if there's a redeemer for us at the end of days.' So they was asking if they'd be saved, ken? Our minister, he has to be delicate. He kens the answer, but he'll not risk angering these trows. So he says, 'For a man to get salvation, he needs a soul, and he needs to love God. It's the same with trows, I doubt.' These trows, they say, 'Oh, we love God, yes. But how do we find out about the soul?' 'There's a test: You have to say the Lord's Prayer straight through.' And so these trows all start reciting the Lord's Prayer, but they canna get past 'Our Father,' past the first two words. They canna say God's up in Heaven.

"And so they run from the house yelling and murning and screaming. When the minister goes and looks out after them, he sees the trowie knowe by Huxter Loch's all ablaze. And so if he'd any uncertainty on this point of theology before, he doesna now. Whatever's happening with the trows come Doomsday, they dunna have souls, and they'll not be saved."

All this talk of religion wore on me. I do not care for their god either way.

But the words burn a little, like the brush of a nettle, no matter how often I hear them. When their monks and priests first came to these islands, they made homes in the faraway places, the rocks out in the sea. They too were attacked by their god, made to suffer for him in their loneliness.

Their god, nameless to me, dying rooted to a tree—and choosing rebirth. The futility. I cannot say whether it is right – assuming, like them, that right and wrong exist – to live for and in the present. If I were one of them, I could perhaps see the appeal of living for the past. But living for the future? When the future comes, there will always be a future beyond it.

"And how are your studies coming?" John asked.

"I can take as long as I need."

"When I was young—"

"There's no pressure. It's not like a Bachelor's degree. So many people start PhDs they never finish, you can keep the university happy just by writing to them every few weeks. It lets them think they've still got you."

"For your own sake..."

"I keep busy."

John began filling his pipe, his thoughts elsewhere. The young man sensed it and gave him time to broach the subject, whatever it was, on his own. They passed a minute in silence.

"You're studying trows. But... Would you put faith in it?"

"No," the young man said quickly. "But we all get the feeling sometimes, right? That there's something or other in the room with us or that we've seen or heard something? I don't try to explain that. I don't have an explanation for that. That's why I'm only interested in the stories."

John thought a moment. "It can't be easy. What with the research. You have to be careful not to be drawn too far in."

The young man laughed.

"No, now, I say this as one who cares about you. It's not healthy to think too much on these things."

"But they don't exist. There's no danger."

"Aye, aye. Right enough. Though there's things you can make exist if you dwell on them. Take Graham. Now, I wouldn't say he *believes* things, ken? But he's been known to say things. Say about what he's seen. And that's not healthy."

The young man leaned forward. "The things he's said: Did he say them before he took to drink? Or only after? There's a difference in causality."

"That I cannot say. That I cannot say. But Graham's not a well man, Innes. It would do to be careful with him, for both your sakes. And though he and I were never what you'd call friends, we fished together, and what with my Laurie and his

May, I've a certain stake in it, ken?"

"I know." The young man slurped his coffee.

★

THE GREY SEAL CORPSE lay sprawled on the beach, hollowed out by animals. Scraps of hide had dried taut over its ribs, teeth jutted from its fleshless muzzle, and its eye sockets were empty and dumb. The seal was smiling the constrained grin of a mort-head, which has seen death in its awe and been transfixed.

The night was premature. Its afterbirth of stars spilled out across space where the sun ought to have been. Or clouds, at least, to mute the eternity of faceless aether.

Oh, you would not know the horror of it, not at all, unless you too had stared for millennia at the same faceless sky, seen it in winter and trembled at its hollow epochs, seen its summer mask yet known the nothingness that lay behind. Only then would you understand. And that is the secret of this world. Those who came before? They are a joke perpetuated upon the weak defenceless things that crawl and reek of peat. I do not believe in them, I think. I am almost certain they are a lie. Nothing came before. We that are are time's pinnacle.

"Would you like a cup of tea?" the young man asked.

"Could do that maybe," said Graham.

They left the beach and walked up the slope to the cottage. The seal remained behind, grinning on the rocks.

I Have Not Answered

The young man set the kettle on the old stove, and they listened to the rushing gas flame.

"You grew up here."

"Moved away when I was sixteen. House up the road was built in '77. We was all building things those days."

"John Millar said your father found a body in the cellar."

"Did he now? Well, I dunna ken. My father told stories. What was true and what wasna, it wasna always easy to say."

The young man poured water into the mugs, and the tea bags bobbed to the top—like a pair of gas-bloated seal corpses, I thought. But the thought was so bizarre, I stopped thinking it even before the young man had begun pouring the milk.

"Not once has du said a word about May." Graham took a sip, the tea bag swilling up against his lips.

The young man fished the tea bag out of his cup and dropped it into the sink. "How's that?"

"Du's never mentioned my daughter."

"Oh, I know her."

"Du doesna have to say it for me to know. Nor does she. But the way she speaks about dee."

"What way is that?"

"She kens it too, boy."

"What does she know?"

Graham exhaled loudly. "It's no problem for me, ken? These things happen. But her and Laurie is aye awful close. Always has been. There's nothing for dee, boy."

"I don't know what you mean."

"Does du no? That's fine then."

For a time, neither of them spoke.

The young man said, "Aren't I the one who's meant to be asking about you? Your innermost secrets?"

"Du can ask. Doesna mean du'll be answered."

"When did it happen? You know…?" The young man made a vague gesture.

"There's nothing *happened*. And besides, that's no a question du'll get answered."

"I have a story."

"Du and dy stories."

"It's a Shetland story. You may have heard it before. It comes from a song."

Graham said nothing.

"There was a king named Orfeo. One day, the king of the trows stole his wife. Orfeo set out after them, following their tracks. He followed them for years and years until the tracks ended at a big grey stone lying up against a hill. Orfeo took out his bagpipes, and because his heart was heavy, he played notes of sorrow. Then he played notes of joy and notes of madness. The boulder shifted, and a voice from the hill said he should come in and be among the people there. Once Orfeo got inside, he again played the notes of sorrow, joy, and madness. The king of the trows asked what reward he'd have for his playing. Orfeo said he wanted his wife back. So the king of the trows returned his wife and said they'd each rule their own country like before. And that's how the story ends."

I Have Not Answered

Graham nodded.

"Have you heard it before?"

"The stories du tells is all the same. All end the same. Thinks du only on redemption? Other tales end different."

"Without redemption? End sadly? Do you know a story like the one I just told?"

"Du canna understand. There's nothing *happens*."

For some reason, I thought about the seal corpse on beach. They never really finally disappear, you know. In the end, when there are only bones left, the bones just stay there. Beaches are littered with bones. Stones shatter them, creatures devour the marrow and gnaw away the ligaments, but in the end, they are always bones. That is their eternity.

★

THE YOUNG MAN plucked a tuft of wool off the fence. "I'll collect more and knit you a shawl."

May laughed. "Du canna knit, can dee?"

"I can learn."

"*I* can't even knit. It's no right du comes here and does all the Shetland things better than wis."

He disentangled another tuft and placed it in his pocket. "Just like the Scots have always done? Stealing land from the poor, trusting Shetlanders…"

"Stealing wir fish."

"Stealing your women."

"You never!"

"How would you like your shawl?" He traced an outline across her back and chest. "Come around like this?"

"That's how old ladies wear them. *Wore* them. Back when they was yet living." She zipped her jacket all the way up and shivered at its warmth against the November chill.

"Oh, no. It'll be the height of fashion. *Innes Pitmedden's Hand-Collected Shawls*. They'll come from all over the isles to see them. From Edinburgh even. You can be my model."

"Can I that? 'Oh, the gallant Scotsman's so beneficent! And me, a simple farm girl!'"

The young man looked across Loch of Sung and out to Foula. The clouds glowed silver, and a piece of wintry noon light shone obliquely on the island, setting all its details in sharp relief. "Do you ever feel it's watching you?"

"It's an island. No more. Du should go there. Take the ferry frae Walls. That'll break the spell."

"Will it?"

"Foula's no the same when du's there. It's just hills and grass and sheep shit like everywhere else. Take the ferry."

"The Kame is meant to be stunning."

"Da Kame's stunning frae a distance."

"You're not worried about me? I've walked on cliffs before."

"Just the rocks can get loose. And it'll no do wir tourism industry any favours if a visiting folklorist goes over the edge."

He leaned over and kissed her. It was very quick, and by the time she had gained full presence, it was over. She seemed unsure what to do. From the look on her face, I think that, had he still been kissing her, she would have pushed him gently away. Now that he was done, she was helpless.

"And what was that for?" she said.

"For taking care I don't go over the Kame."

"If du's so easily grateful..."

She was already smiling again, and I felt this made him happy, though I could not be sure. They can be unpredictable.

"In Buddhist tradition," he said, "there's something called a hungry ghost."

May laughed. "I kens a few of them."

"It's not a ghost like you'd maybe think of a ghost. It's like... When a person dies, if his life has been filled with desire, he could be reborn a hungry ghost. Reincarnation. And a hungry ghost always wants what it can't have. It's obsessed with something. So it could be it's always hungry. And its neck, maybe, is thin as a needle while its stomach is large as a mountain. So it can't eat, right? Or maybe, as soon as it touches what it desires, that thing explodes into flame."

She was no longer smiling.

He turned back to Foula. "I think it *is* watching though."

"So long as it only watches. There's no harm in that."

"But if...?"

"That wouldna be good. It doesna fit inta the way of things, Innes. Things are good as they are."

"I'm not so sure."

The fey streamers went up over Foula—gold, then blue.

I have never learned what the colours betoken. They were lifted on a low wind and carried in our direction. I lost them as they neared shore and did not see where they came down.

He said, "Sometimes I think it's already too late."

"But it's not dy choice to make."

"No."

She put a hand on his shoulder. "Things'll be better, yeah?"

It is a queer thing, but my body was buzzing. My stomach ached too, which was strange as I had eaten a decent lunch a few hours earlier, a tin of mackerel from Brian Neely's larder.

There were tears in his eyes.

He turned and kissed her, but she pushed him gently away. She saw his tears.

Then she drew his head to hers and kissed him, nipping his lower lip in that odd little way they sometimes do.

It was distinctly unpleasant. My fingertips felt set to explode. I do not recall having had this sensation before.

But one forgets so many things.

He ran his hand down her back and cupped it around a buttock, holding her close as they kissed.

She waited a second, then nudged his arms away and took a step backward.

"Things are good as they are."

He turned to Foula. "The shawl will be blue. To match your eyes."

★

I Have Not Answered

THE YOUNG MAN held the nozzle up to his nose and inhaled. Mixed blossoms, honey, and thyme. He had his eyes closed and stood in the bathroom, waiting for something to happen.

Nothing happened.

But when he went back into the main room, he saw the scarf lying on the bed. I had picked out a red and black one. It was among those she wore most often. Before taking it from the house, I had sprayed a puff of orange blossom perfume on it. It would provide him with more data that way.

He stood by the writing table, absolutely still, eyes open, trying not to blink. It was a strange reaction since he had, of course, seen the scarf many times before and does not usually react to scarves in this manner. But he regarded it as a foreign object, some alien thing washed onto the beach after a storm.

"May?" he whispered.

I held off the urge to laugh. He had said this thing so softly that even if she had been with him in the room, she would not have heard it. They are strange like that, saying things to other people that are not meant to be heard.

"May," he said more loudly. It echoed off the far wall.

He walked to the bed and rubbed a corner of the scarf between his fingers, as he sometimes does with tufts of wool. But then, the scarf is woollen, so there is a certain logic to it.

"I trusted you."

There was a scrabbling noise outside the west window. The young man heard it too, for he went over and looked out, seeing nothing. I would not have looked myself, even if he had not stood in my way. But he kept looking. I knew Foula would be there in moonlight. Its view would be blocked by the head of Murnin Kame, but if you stare at the hillside hard enough, you can sense Foula looming behind it.

He turned from the window and looked through me into the darkened corner of the room.

"Why did you do it?"

It gave me a little thrill of pleasure to imagine he was talking to me. So I indulged in the imagination for a moment.

"Your life was fine. Why did you do it?"

The wind picked up outside and rattled the windows.

"It's not wrong to love. You can love without desire."

I began feeling a bit uncomfortable standing there with him looking straight through me, so I moved aside a few paces.

"It will be awakened. In all the world, there's nothing that won't be awakened." He was rasping, his voice hoarse. "Even the undone years. Awakened. The wool on the fence at Finnigarth, the seal on the beach, your research. All awakened. You've been down paths you don't even know. Love is the path. You are love. You could destroy them all. Then there'd just be you and her. They'd be dust, and you'd belong to her."

I had known from the beginning he was unlike the others.

Tears were in his eyes. "You trusted yourself. Why?"

That night, he had a dream. The wind was roaring outside like a bull seal, and in his dream, he woke in bed. Rain smashed against the west window. The sea had come up over the cliffs, and the fields were all awash, waves crashing against

I Have Not Answered

the side of the cottage. Foula loomed black to the southwest. Dozens of grey seals raised their bodies from the ocean that had come ashore, and they all sang out in that heartrendingly melancholic way of theirs, as though mourning someone.

As though someone had died.

A cluster of seals approached the window, holding in their flippers a little white thing, at first indistinct. But as they came closer, crying all the while, the details were filled, and I could see that what they held was a strange little skeleton, lifted into the air like an offering. Its skull was bright and white and was like that of a human baby, but below the neck, the bones were as those of a small seal pup.

The young man woke with tears in his eyes.

★

"Do you know the story of King Orfeo?" the young man asked.

"A story..." May sighed.

"Haven't heard it," Laurie said.

"Has it a king, then?" asked May.

"That. And bagpipes. A man's wife is taken by the trows, but he gets her back by playing the bagpipes."

"First time for everything," said Laurie.

"I kens a story," May said. "And this one – Dr Professional Folklorist – is said to be true." She spoke quickly, forestalling interruption. "There's these two men living on either side of a firth. They dunna like each other overmuch, and it's no helping that there's whole a pack of trows living nearby. This one man, when the trows gets to be too much for him, he takes out his fiddle and plays at them. I kens that trows sometimes like fiddling, but other times, they dunna. So this man scares them off to the other side of the firth. Of course, that's no making his neighbour happy. And so this other man, he plays the pipes. So when the first man fiddles the trows over the firth, the second man pipes them all the way back again. And back and forth, all through the night. That's what they said about these two men lived over by Gruting."

"That's a good one," Laurie said.

May kissed his cheek. "At least someone appreciates me."

"This story about King Orfeo, it's a Shetland story," the young man said.

"Not with bagpipes?" Laurie said. "No."

"There's another very similar story, and it's from Denmark. There's a song to it, just like 'King Orfeo' is actually a ballad. It's called 'The Power of the Harp'."

"It's no that with the girl's bones?" May asked.

"Not at all. Completely different. But the same too. And I'm wondering if there's another story you might remember if you heard it."

"OK," said Laurie.

The young man sang in his own voice, with little conviction.

Herr Vellemand's built a bridge so wide,
Twelve knights rode at his maiden's side.

I Have Not Answered

But when on the bridge she rode,
Her horse into the stream stumbled.

Herr Vellemand to his squire speaks,
"The golden harp you must seek."
Herr Vellemand played so soft a hush,
No bird flitted in the brush.

He struck the harp so awful hard,
They heard it all across the world.
The bark broke off the old oak tree,
And horns from cattle roaring free.

The bark broke off the old birch,
The steeple fell from Mary's Church.
Then he struck the harp with harm,
He struck his bride from the troll's arms.

He struck the harp down to the base,
The troll and the maid rise up in haste.
His sword Herr Vellemand stoutly drew,
He struck and hewed that troll in two.

"All I'm reminded of is the other song," Laurie said.

"See, there are some of these songs that are quite alike. And some end happily like this one, but others end sadly."

"Is it a sad song du's wanting? Or a happy one?" asked May.

"I'm open to suggestions."

"Du should do happy songs. It suits dee."

Laurie looked at May with annoyance.

The young man sat in the chair by the coffee table. May and Laurie sat on the sofa, which gave me an unpleasant feeling.

"Why," said May, "doesna the lassie die seeing as she's been with the troll? Du's insisted before that they die. But maybe du canna keep dy stories straight."

"The fairy took her. It wasn't her choice, as it was with the girl in the song about the merman."

"That, and she didn't have sex with him," said Laurie.

The young man laughed. "That might've had something to do with it too."

"Is it sex then?" said May. "Is that the meaning du's been reading inta all wir tales?"

"I never said that."

"He didn't say that," Laurie said.

The young man reached into his pocket. He had a tuft of wool there, and I suspect he was rubbing it between his fingers.

"No..." said May, suddenly thoughtful.

All three of them seemed uncomfortable.

"Has du no coffee in the house, Laurie?" May said abruptly. "Is du forgetting dy manners? With an esteemed guest."

Laurie stood up. "I'll make some coffee, I think." He smiled as best he could and left the room. The young man looked at the bookshelf. They were quiet for a few moments.

"I'm sorry," May said softly.

I Have Not Answered

The young man turned to her, his face somewhat cruel. "I've heard worse. They say all sorts of things about folklorists."

"That's no what I meant."

"I understand."

"I shouldna have—the other day."

"Things are good as they are?"

"Yeah." She folded her arms.

Water was running in the kitchen, and Laurie was clattering around loudly.

"Anyway, you're taking it too seriously," the young man said. "It was just a moment. It's not like I go around thinking about it." He paused. "It was a misunderstanding."

She looked down. "That's all right then."

Laurie came in with the coffee.

"Smells wonderful strong," the young man said.

"Extra strong for you," said Laurie. "All the coffee you drink at folk's houses. It's killed your taste buds, man. You should drink tea instead."

"I'm not the one who asked for coffee," the young man said, glancing at May.

Laurie frowned.

May was angry. "But it's what dee wanted."

"You're speaking in riddles again." Laurie threw up his arms. "How you two understand each other is beyond me."

"Du's no missing anything. I dunna understand the half of it myself. But it's polite to pretend."

Laurie stalked out and started washing up in the kitchen.

The young man looked concerned, and I think he considered following after him.

But he did not.

They are odd, with their passions and torments and lies. So much they say, they do not mean. I have never said a thing I do not mean. Dissimulation is not in my nature. For them, it is natural. And when they do speak truthfully, even that is a lie, for they are incapable of saying what is true without masking it to make it appear more like lying. It is fear, I think. Like the fear of someone learning your true name, which can be used against you. There are so many words for so few things and yet also so much that is wordless. They would be happier, these creatures, if they did not talk at all.

Only the young man is consistent. With him, it is not a lie, for everyone knows what he is. He carries a digital audio recorder and notebooks. He makes maps of people. It is not a lie when everyone knows you are acting. They could not expect him to enter their homes and act out something besides his true self. For his true self is an observer, and an observer is like a chameleon when he is observing. But people appreciate it, I think, because there is a certainty to it. They can be certain he does not really care. A mirror does not care what it reflects. It is nice to have something to trust in.

Laurie returned from the kitchen. He was stuck, I suppose, since it was his house, so he could not really leave. But he was unhappy. It is their urge to possess things and keep them for themselves. Yet the young man, that rock in the ocean—

he belongs to everybody. If Laurie were not such a dumb animal thing, he would not be jealous. He would know that he too could be researched, if only he were interesting enough.

Laurie clapped his hands. "Hate to break this up, but I've some work to get done. Follow up on our digital accounts programme. I'm going South for a seminar next week."

A few minutes later, May and the young man stood outside, cold coming at them from the west. The land just before was illuminated by light from the windows, but otherwise it was dark.

Clouds covered the moon and stars, masking the terror of the eternal sky.

The young man glanced at May and laughed.

"Let's go then," she said.

They walked up the track, then on the road west. Snow began falling, the first of the season. These were flakes, not just dots of ice, but the ground was too warm for them to stick.

"In parts of Japan," the young man said, "they dress up, put on masks, and go out at night pretending to be demons."

Their boots clomped down on the asphalt, as so many pairs of boots have clomped over this land before them.

"That's how they propitiate the demons. By becoming demons themselves."

They were walking quickly now.

"I dunna care about dy demons."

"But the demons may care about you."

"They can care all they want. It'll no make any difference."

"Not to you."

May stopped walking. "Yeah. And I should be taking advice frae one that's nought better to do than stand around with my father staring at a dead seal."

"He's a good man."

"Aye. A great man, is my father."

"He understands. With the seal."

"He understands nothing. And the sooner du gives up on whatever du's after, the better. Du'll no get anything frae him du couldna get frae any drunk anywhere in the world."

The young man was trembling. "He has secrets."

"Aye. Live in the same house with the man twenty-two years, then du can tell me all about his secrets."

"He knows—"

"He kens nothing. He kens he likes your drink. That's all."

A car was coming up behind them from the village, so she took his arm and pulled him over with her onto the verge.

"Du's better than that, Innes. Feeding drink to an alcoholic. Thinks du he'd tell dee the story du's after even if he kenned it? He'd no do it. As long as he has a thing du wants, du belongs to him, ken? He can do with dee just as he likes."

"It's more complicated than that. I have training."

"Oh, training. Of course."

"I have experience."

"This is no place for dee. If du has to bide in Shetland, then go do it in town. My mother and I won't miss dee."

I Have Not Answered

I was angry. She did not understand, is unworthy of his research. I might have killed her right then and there had he not been present. I know of a blade in the rocks, near where there are lights in the hill at night. I would have cut her throat and spilled her into the deep peat, leaving just a finger behind on the blacktop, for a bird to find, or some passing traveller.

He clenched his fists.

"That's right. Du's angry. Fine. It's no my concern. Go off and interview the whole bloody island. I dunna care anymore. Whatever du's wanting, du'll no find it. Because it's no here." She poked him in the chest. "Soul. That's what du's lacking. What kinda man goes months on end trying to hear about trowies? Ken? It's madness. Mad as my father."

She turned and jogged off into the darkness, her boots clacking rhythmically on the road. The young man looked after her, then looked back the way they had come. He seemed to be considering going back to Laurie's house.

This May, she is a blighted crawling thing in the muck.

But I have known another way, once, half-remembered, with shining black hair and a harp of gold.

But May is nothing. Worse than nothing, for she does harm. She is a rat in the walls, feasting on the house, devouring the ligaments that keep it standing. Most animals may be suffered, for they do no real harm. But not rats. Rats should be killed.

The young man did not go back to Laurie. He shot off in May's direction, moving quickly despite his heavy boots. She must have heard him because she began running in earnest.

The young man caught up with her in the darkest shadow of Murnin Kame, where the road comes in close by the hillside. He reached out for her, but she dodged to the side—rather too far, in fact, for she slipped on the verge and stumbled up against the start of the slope.

He pounced, had her pinned down before she could react.

There was a large stone embedded in the hill just beside them, and I could sense beneath it a lethal gleaming sharpness. Just to reach out. He could have held it in his hand.

He tore off her red cap and grabbed her short, black hair. Then, still straddling her, he released her arms and propped himself up an elbow, holding her hair in the other hand and pulling her head slightly toward him.

"Kiss me," he said.

She punched him in the face.

The spell was broken. He sprang up, trembling. "May..." His nose began to bleed.

She got to her feet, picked up her cap, and glared at him a moment before jogging off toward her house.

The young man stood there, the snow, heavier now, falling against him.

He wiped his hand under his nose and saw the blood chill against the back of his fingers. But it was very dark, so what he really saw, I cannot say.

"May."

There was a noise close behind me.

By instinct, I spun around.

I Have Not Answered

There was nothing to see. But I thought, maybe, I could hear it breathing. Whether it could see me, I did not know.

Just in case, I stood very still.

Although I heard the young man resume his walk, slowly now, I did not dare move to follow, lest I turn my back on the thing in the darkness.

Perhaps it would turn its back on me first.

★

FOR THE NEXT WEEKS, the young man hardly left the cottage, just went out once to fetch things from the shop.

He did not even visit the beach. The decomposed seal corpse no doubt remains, cold and dead, but with living things sheltering in its wrecked carcass, skittering among the salt-bleached bones like tiny rats, gnawing away at what they can.

Graham came to the cottage three times and knocked on the door, tried peering through the curtained windows. But the young man did not answer, so he eventually left. Though Graham could, I suspect, have got a key with no trouble.

The young man grew pale and thin. He barely ate. Sometimes just a single nut over the course of a day. He sat naked on the floor for hours on end, all folded up like a flower, his eyes closed as if in sleep.

He was not asleep.

But he did dream. Or saw things resembling dreams.

The air in the cottage was foul with that awful scented smoke of his, smouldering, always smouldering on the white flower plate. It nearly drove me mad, that smoke.

His breaths were shallow as he sat on the floor. Sometimes, I feared him dead and went right up close to check. Yet still his pitted stomach rose and fell. And it was especially at these times, when his breathing was so hardly there, and I came up to him, that his dream eyes would join with mine.

Once, through his eyes, I saw a dark emaciated man sitting at the base of a great tree. So thin was he that his ribs nearly broke through the skin, and his head was trim as a skull. He sat just as the young man sat, still, near death, for what seemed an eternity, so that the lifetimes I have lived were as nothing compared with the time I spent watching that dark man beneath the tree. Eras of man rose and fell as I watched.

But then. A rushing of air. And all the trees about him broke into flower, and the grasses themselves glowed with inner light, and the man beneath the tree, twig-thin, was enwraptured by vines, blossoming out with blue flowers. The man opened his eyes, a third eye appearing in the centre of his brow, splitting him down the middle, cracking him in two, and the air was filled with a rush of light that burned the vision away.

And the young man sat there panting, naked on the floor, his own eyes open. But still he did not rise. For days and days, he rose only to light a new cone of sick smoke, to take a nut or a sip of water in the kitchen.

I Have Not Answered

I wondered at times if this would be the end of him. Would his will, so strong and vital, starve into nothingness on the floor? And it occurred to me that it was in my power to help him rise. I could remind him of his power and his will.

So, loath though I was to leave him, vulnerable and alone, I sometimes went out and brought him keepsakes of May. A sock, a pencil, her red cap. And whenever he found one of these things at his feet upon opening his eyes after a sitting session, he would stare at it for a long time, as if he did not recognise it. Quite possibly, he did not recognise the pencil. But then maybe he did, for when he saw it, he said, "May."

But anyway. He would stare at these items. Then he would place them in a little box he kept beneath the bed. Occasionally, he would get up from the floor, take out the box, and turn the things over in his hands. He placed in this box too some bits of driftwood and tufts of wool, which is very odd, for these things have no connection with May.

But they are quite unpredictable. At times, he would speak softly to himself in a language I could not comprehend. In these mumblings, I fancied I could hear speech from the time of those who came before. But this was just a fancy, for I am led to believe that there was no speech at all in that time, just the monotonous beating of drums and tuneless mad pipings.

This was a difficult period for me. It is not, you will understand, in my nature always to stay in one place. I yearned to be among the sheep or to look at the dead seal on the beach. Once, I will admit, when I was on my way back with something of May's, I ascended Murnin Kame for no reason but to see the weak winter sunrise. And when I reached the spine of the hill, the sunrise soured and curdled in my eyes, for I felt a thing akin to guilt.

Which, you should know, is not a thing I ever feel.

The languishment of these days settled upon me. It is strange how centuries can pass almost without notice, but a few weeks in winter can be interminable. I believe there may have been this thing in my soul – or whatever you would call it – that they refer to as *longing*. I almost think I longed for the days when the Northmen came, when there were killings and things, and all was in flux. Back then, one could nearly imagine that times would change, that the revolutions of man might be mirrored in the dull heavens. But the stars were just as dumb then too. Change is a delusion among men because they cannot see far enough behind and before to know that all is levelled in the end.

But these things he says, in that strange language. It is funny how familiar it seems. There is something called a *kindred spirit*, which is a thing that is very like another thing in all its essentials. This young man, he is unlike the rest. How much speech have I heard in my days? It is a bubble in the burn, which passes and breaks, unmissed. Yet in his speech, I feel something of myself, a cadence, my own spirit. He is a man, so like other men. But he is also otherwise. He understands the monstrosity of eternity, the waves of millennia that crash into one another, pinning one another down, drowning in infinite union.

I Have Not Answered

Someday he will go out again into the world. He will leave me and, in leaving, will do great things, through the epochs.

But I shall have known him here, in this cottage, by this beach, at the base of this hillside where there are lights.

★

THE YOUNG MAN sat on the floor, and I thought back to how Paul Stevens had once sat before the fire in this very house and how they had all gathered there to hear him tell it.

The laird in Sandness, he's after building a little church.

Over at the voe here. Beside the kame.

And so all the folk round about has to help. Has to build the church, see? And maybe they're no ower blide to do it, for there's work enough on the croft. But they has to do it.

So they start building.

But they dunna get far. No.

Every night, what happens, it's all torn down. Whatever they's built during the day. Gets ripped down at night. No matter how low the wall, just gets knocked down, see?

And so, the men, they go to Sandness, see the laird. Say, 'Canna build the church there. Trows won't have it and is tearing it down. Try moving it maybe.'

But the laird, he'll no listen. Wants the church built right there, beside the voe. Won't let the men rest till it's done.

'What do we do?' asks one.

'Ask Old Leena,' says another.

So they go and ask Old Leena. 'Find a man what's never sinned and put him in the wall. Have him seal himself up.'

'Wall himself up?'

She says, 'Has to do it himself, mind.'

'How do we get him out again?'

'Don't get him out again. But the trows will keep away.'

And so they're wondering if any among them's never sinned.

'I stole from the poor box once.'

'I spied on the minister's wife bathing.'

'I went fishing on a Sunday.'

And so they've all sinned.

'What about a baby?' says one. 'Oh, we'll find a peerie baby and put it in the wall.'

But that's no good. Baby canna build the wall himself, see?

'What about Tammie Brains?' there's one says.

Tammie's no too clever, see?

Canna hardly tie his shoes, can Tammie. So if he's sinned, he'll no really have known what he's done. So it'll no really have been a sin. But he's awful strong.

So they get Tammie.

'Du, Tammie,' they say, 'we need help.'

'Sure,' says Tammie.

'There's a key missing. Key to Paradise. We's lost it.'

'Lost it where?'

'Lost it under that pile of stones.'

'Oh, sure,' says Tammie, 'I'll find it.'

So Tammie.

I Have Not Answered

He climbs atop this heap of stones lying up against a wall they's just built. And he starts shifting them. Stacks them up, half circle, around the pile. Looking for that key.

'Has du found the key?'

'No, I've no found the key.'

'Then keep on stacking.'

And he keeps on stacking. Till he's midway through the pile. And he's built a wall up around him, all up to his waist. 'Still canna see the key."

'Oh,' they say, 'oh, it's there alright. Just keep stacking.'

And he keeps stacking. Keeps stacking till it's up to his head. 'It's dark in here now. Maybe so dark as I canna see the key.'

'Du'll find it. Just feel around with your hands.'

And so he stacks some more. And soon the wall's so high as he canna put more stones on top but has to start building a roof, see? 'I canna find the key,' says Tammie, 'and there's just one stone left.'

'Oh, it must be under that stone. Check under that stone.'

Tammie puts that last stone atop his head, and he's all sealed in. 'Has du found the key?'

But he doesna answer.

So they shout, 'Has du found the key?'

And Tammie, he shouts back. But it comes out no louder than a whisper to them on the other side of the wall. 'I found the key.' He's shouting, but he sounds ever so far off. 'I found the key.'

And that night, the walls is left standing. And the trows didna bother the church anymore after that.

And that's how there's got to be that little church beside the voe.

Part III

DEMON, I HAVE BEEN CALLED, and angel half-fallen, child of Eve and child of Cain, son of the Watchers and witch's familiar, Pict and Finn, and god half-forgotten.

I have been called all these things, but not once have I answered. For to answer the call is to put yourself in their power. There are names and books that by my nature I must fear, symbols from which I must shrink—or be withered, turned to dust, and as dust remain, conscious yet crumbled upon the earth.

Still, no church or churchman has conquered me.

And so, since our time's beginning, I have dwelt in this country, moved through the meadows and moved through the wastes. I have made paths and found paths to follow.

How many times have I passed by one of my fellows and been blind to its passing? How many fates have I failed to touch? Venturing though through hills and down black tunnels, into the earthy groins where ancient kings rot and

I Have Not Answered

seasons pass in centuries. And at the end of every track lie those who came before—mindless and unyielding, the utter limit to endeavour. For such as me, there is no end.

And yet not once have I answered.

But you see, this one is different.

I had a sense of something, so I went out.

And later, still, wet from the rain, I stooped, touched his shoulder, and whispered, "Go to the beach."

He groaned but remained a naked flower on the floor.

"Go to the beach."

The young man opened his eyes and gasped. It was the gasp of a dead thing that thinks it is alive.

The wind roared outside like a grey bull seal.

He was instantly alert. Without pausing a moment, he pulled on his clothes, which hung loose about his thinness, and went out into the night.

The sea was heavy, breaking up against the cliffs, yet he ignored it and headed down the dark slope through the rain. He began to run. His movements were jerky and strange, famished as he was and so unaccustomed to physical exertion. And yet he ran, his motions akin to those of a long-legged wading bird with broken wings.

He came over the crest of turf and rushed onto the shingle. Waves reached far up the beach, and the sea was higher than was its right. Out in the middle of the beach, waist-deep in sea, maniacally withstanding the tug and press of the waves, a figure stood facing the dead ocean.

The young man went straight in, jolting from the shock of the frigid waters. He was so thin, the stream slid around and past, and like the stalk of some water flower, the ocean could not move him. He stepped forward undaunted, slipped, went under, and somehow righted himself, continuing toward the shadow in the waves.

"Graham!" he shouted.

It has been four generations since I have heard a man shout so deep and from his centre.

The figure did not turn.

"Graham!" The young man reached, grabbed his shoulder.

Graham looked out to pale masked Foula, on which a clutch of moonlight shone amidst the storm, a bastion of white peace. He did not react to the touch. The young man tried pulling him toward the shore, but Graham was tall and heavy, and his legs were set against it.

The sea beat the young man down again. He stumbled but did not fall. He screamed, "I must know how it ends!"

Graham turned away from Foula, glanced at the young man, then turned back.

Foula. I felt its presence then, unmistakable, a vibration in the air, ocean ringing against the Kame, cliffs without end in the beginning. I could have fallen – hateful rock! – into that dark gap and so been lost. But I had presence and withstood. Drowned men, do what you will. Whales and mangled boats and bloated songs upturned. All nothing to me, save the undone years. My harp of gold and a cup at your lips so that

I Have Not Answered

you may drink. Oh, I have drunk deeply and have laughed. What is this ocean to me? It is provisional. It does not bind. I am a rock rising above.

The young man got in front of him, lowered his head, and charged into Graham's stomach, forcing him back. They both fell, but the young man was on top, and he worked with the waves to keep Graham's head above water and tug him out into the shallow surf. Graham lay there, immobile without the waves. I knew that the young man could not do it on his own, so I lent him my strength and helped as he took Graham beneath the arms and pulled him up the beach.

The storm was unabated when we reached the house. The young man pounded on the door. Late though it was, just half a minute passed, and light opened up before him.

Margaret stood there in her nightgown, silhouetted. May was rushing down the stairs behind, the top two buttons of her shirt undone. I saw this vignette in a flash of stillness, an echo of something fated and ancient, branded upon my mind.

Pushing them aside, the young man dragged Graham in from the rain and knelt beside him. "He's cold. God, he's cold."

"What—" began May. And she stopped as she saw the young man's thinness, her father's paleness.

"We've got to get him to hospital." The young man was shouting. Perhaps the sea was still in his ears.

"I'll get the keys," May said.

When she returned, her mother was standing motionless as the young man knelt, stroking Graham's white hair.

"We're ready," said May.

With difficulty, she and the young man lifted Graham into the backseat of the car. The young man climbed in with him.

"Innes," said Margaret blankly, "you'd best get home."

May was already in the driver's seat. "Leave it, Ma. He's the only one can talk with him. Du kens that."

Margaret went around and sat in the passenger's seat.

"He has training," May said, starting the engine.

★

"Why was du there?" asked May.

The young man stared at the wall in Gilbert Bain Hospital. An empty paper cup sat on the table beside him. He had drunk four cups of coffee since they had arrived and had eaten a pot of rice pudding from the little canteen.

"Did du go there with him?"

"No."

May turned away.

"I just—I had a feeling. It's like I knew."

"Fuck." May shook her head.

The young man looked at her. She had been crying.

"I don't know," he said.

"Du held his fucking head in dy lap the whole way over." She stamped a foot. "And how am I supposed to hate dee?"

"I shouldn't."

"Yeah. It's easy now, is it no?"

"There are things I don't understand."

"Yeah."

"He was looking at Foula."

"I dunna give a fuck about bloody Foula."

"Listen." He paused, unable for a moment to continue. "Listen. I don't know where my head was. I can't ask your forgiveness. But what happened isn't in my nature. I'd never. It's like someone else—well, it's lonely out there. You speak to so many people and never really get to know them. An hour with him, two hours with her, transfer the audio files onto the laptop, spend eight hours transcribing, then start again. I guess it's like, you and Laurie, you're the only pieces of reality anchoring me down, right?"

"Is that dy excuse?"

"It's not an excuse. It's not an excuse. I wish I understood. I've tried to understand."

"Why do you do it?"

"Why am I here? Why the research? It's science. It's a thing I need to complete the picture."

She laughed, and there was a note of happiness, if just a little one. "It's madness."

"But there's method to it?"

May reached her arms around his waist and placed her head in the nook of his skeletal neck. He tilted his head to the side so it rested against hers, yet his arms dangled, impotent, as he resisted the urge to hug her back.

She was smiling, but he could not see it.

A nurse came up, and May released him.

"News?" May asked.

"He'll be fine. Your mother's lying down in an empty room." The nurse nodded toward the young man but kept speaking to May. "Your father wants to see him. But if you—"

"And he's every right to see him. This man's saved his life. We can aye feel insulted once Daa's better." She turned to the young man. "Go to him, Innes."

The morning bustle was just beginning, but Graham's room was quiet. The young man took a seat beside the bed. Graham looked up at him vaguely.

The young man leaned forward. "What did you see?"

"All the world from the beginning," Graham whispered.

"That means nothing. What did you see?"

"And there was selkies riding each of the waves."

"There weren't any seals. I didn't see any seals. Besides, they're just animals."

"The end is like the beginning. Du shoulda let me have it."

"I couldn't. You know that."

"Aye, I kens that."

"Was it Foula?"

Graham closed his eyes. "'Was it Foula?' It's nought to do with Foula. That's a symbol. Du's so bloody literal minded."

The young man leaned back. "You know nothing."

"Nought worth knowing."

"Then why?"

"To see if I could learn it. I was drawn."

"To the beginning?"

"Du's no making sense, boy."

"Don't tire yourself." The young man stood and walked toward the door.

"They was there," Graham called out, more loudly.

"No, they weren't. It's a delusion to think things like that care. They don't. Only people care about you. If that."

"Du cares."

"Yes." And then the young man left.

★

THE YOUNG MAN was reinspired, had returned to writing research notes, looking through transcripts, trying to piece together his story. He no longer sat cross-legged on the floor, lit smoke cones, or muttered strange words. It had been right for me to intervene. It had been worth the risk.

Now when he interviews people, it is different. He is colder. He cuts through peoples' lies, exposes their truths, asks about the horrible things they have done, the dreams they had and had forgotten. They have no choice but to answer. His will is sovereign. When he leaves them, he is stronger than when he came. It is a wonderful strength, that, to take someone's truth. His mirror is clearer now, reflecting only that which is important.

But there are other things too. The sounds outside the west window have ceased. There is nothing so strange in this. Yet it is not something you would think, for the young man's mind still seems haunted, troubled by a presence. You can sense the press of the uncanny in his dreams, like the discordant playing of a harp or the mumbling of monotonous idiot pipes. It is an echo of the time of those who came before.

This evening, the young man was in the kitchen, preparing a meal. He sliced an onion, added it to the meat in the pan, boiled potatoes from the day before, added these too. As the food was browning, he looked over his list of people to revisit.

The front door opened in the next room. The young man turned off the gas and spooned the roast beef hash onto a pair of plates. Graham did not even have time to enter the kitchen before the young man was in the main room, setting the food on the writing table. They ate in silence.

When they were done, the young man said, "Now, tell me what you've seen." Saving someone's life prompts a certain boldness.

Graham looked old and tired. "What I've seen."

"Folk say you can see things. That you see more than most." This was an exaggeration. He had heard that Graham saw things that were not there, which is a different matter.

Graham looked down. There was nothing he wished to say. "I was nine years old. It was summer. We was biding a fortnight with family over in Voe."

The young man was silent.

In the midst of this silence, ancient memories came to me. It was to Voe that the flocks had been drawn at the start of our time. Our fleets sailed past hallowed Vementry and into

I Have Not Answered

Swarbacks Minn, skirting the passions of Muckle Roe and Papa Little. We made obsequience at the dome of Linga, dropping sacrifices – bound and gouged – into the Cole Deep, where they were swallowed up by the things beneath. Passage thus granted, the little wicker boats came by Grobsness and entered Olna Firth, her rounded thighs welcoming us to our rest. At the pit of the firth lay the propitious country of Voe. There too we made offerings, consecrating the soil. But other tribes also sought this point, scrabbling up along the Lang Kames, slopping in from the lakes of Lunnasting, and other places besides. As we had already consecrated the earth, the others determined it must be consecrated anew if it were to be a suitable dwelling place for their own races.

"I was up on Laxo Knowe pulling herbs. And it got very bright. I looked up. And then I was scared. Because I saw the Crucifix in the sky. I dunna ken what I associate it with. But I thought, well, my last hour's come, for there was this huge, black, shiny cross in the sky. It was like a death sentence, ken? So a man simply thinks, 'Either the world ends, or I end,' ken? But the world didna end. And I didna end. But it was creepy. Damned creepy."

"Was the cross vertical or horizontal?"

"At sorta an angle. In the east. Out over Whalsay. But I'm guessing as it was more horizontal than vertical."

"Did it cast a shadow?"

"The sun was in the west, so I couldna tell. I didna say to anyone. But it's after, I could things."

"How did you first find out?"

"It's the same evening. I'm in the house. And I see my father's mother go past the window. She's in hospital in town. So I says to father, 'I've just seen Gran.' And he says, 'It musta been her feyness passing.' To the old folk, the feyness was a kinda ghost. But I dunna ken what it should rightly be called. And a few minutes after, the hospital rings to give the news.

"But still I didna tell about the cross. And as time goes, more and more things is happening, and I'm seeing more things. It's no that I can spells or make things happen. It's no that. But I can see things before. Seeing what's going to happen. It's mainly that. And it's no pleasant."

"Are there other things?"

"Other things?"

"Are there things you shouldn't name, maybe?"

"Them that fished useta have different names for everything. Otherwise it was unlucky."

"I mean things in the hills?"

"Folk told stories. But I dunna believe it." Graham scowled. "Though there's more as we ken in Heaven and on Earth."

"Are they dangerous?"

"Folk said they was dangerous. Folk said."

"What hidden things can you see? Can you tell about me?"

"I dunna want to go there. No with dee. It's no a thing as can be done on command."

"No." The young man paused. "But I'd like to find out."

"Du's asking if I'll tell about dee? That's no a place I'll go."

I Have Not Answered

"Why? Is it something about me?"

"It's nought about dee. Not everything's about dee."

"Something about what's happening with me?"

Graham closed his eyes.

"What's happening?" the young man asked.

"A man can be troubled though nought's wrong. Times are, a man's just troubled. And that's that."

"Am I troubled?"

"Does du feel troubled?"

"Yes."

"Well, then. Du's answered it dyself." Graham stood up. "But I've kept dee from dy work long enough. And I must be getting on. So good of dee to have me over."

"So good of you," the young man said, "to visit."

★

As I came up the walk, I heard them shouting inside the house. Laurie went out and slammed the door. Most likely, she was standing in his kitchen, looking foolish.

At the end of the path, Laurie glanced in either direction. He could go up by Murnin Kame, but that would take him where she would be headed. If he walked to the village, he might meet people. He could go toward Walls, but why would he want to? I assume this is what he was thinking.

He struck out across the field, sodden and dark though it was. The sheep, accustomed to him, moved aside to make way. The bulk of Stourbrough Hill rose against him to the north, concealing the stars. He made toward the ruined house ahead and to the left. Coming into the shelter of its west wall, he looked back behind him. Stars were shining to the southeast.

Their passions are strange. Love is one of their pretences.

"They can both fucking go to hell," Laurie said.

It is not in my nature to say these things. There is a power that stops me from going beyond a point.

He picked up a stone and threw it at the half wall opposite. The stone bounced off in futility. There were tears in his eyes. They glistened with the light of stars.

"You would do anything. Anything."

Really, they are all alike. One observes them to keep the boredom off, not out of affection. Not as they feel for each other. But nor is there hatred. Just an unchangeable condition.

"Every one of them. Can't stand it."

Their words are without meaning, flowing to nowhere, like bubbles in the burn. But perhaps there is a truth, deeper than they comprehend.

For are they not broken reflections of those who came before, constructed in their image by those who worshipped as gods those who came before? They may be ancient beyond their fathoming.

"But you love her. You always have."

I have thought of a girl sometimes and seen her face before me, foreign and strange, brimming with gold. Her lips taste of blood and wine. The music is in me.

I Have Not Answered

Then the vision fades, and I am alone. It is like waking in a dream, that gap between consciousness and what is left behind.

"It may be time to move on."

And as for May, a mere animal, without meaning past her own existence. Let her and Laurie have their animal desires, their digital accounts, their babies, their pensions. It is no concern of mine. They are nothing to me. When they pass, I shall not miss them. Their fates do not touch me, if they are fated for anything at all. Someday, the young man will leave her and do great things.

It is maddening how the world appears guided by such trifles. But it is only appearance. They are powerless beyond their own point. They look to the sky and gather stars into shapes, read their trajectories from those of distant suns, not realising truth is all hollow and echoes back their own words.

Which are without meaning.

They believe that somewhere there shines a sun especially for them, that it exists to make their plants and beasts grow so that they may eat. They are mad. If I were to destroy one, I would not know which to choose, which to choose first.

It stands in the lee of a broken-down wall, whimpering because it is in pain. It whines its passions like a crawling thing. At least the crawling things whine for their lost gods. It just whines for the loss of another animal. It is ignorant of the world beyond its little circle of knowledge, where there are things that have seen the beginning and will see the end. It is pathetically circumscribed. It would be happier if it were dead.

I know a place where there is a blade in the rocks.
At times, I have even held it myself.

★

JOHN MILLAR POINTED to a hump, barely perceptible, on the bulging headland. "That's a burial mound. There were stories about it in the old days, I think."

"What kind of stories?" asked the young man.

Every time I am up here, I feel this place was once my home. I am not attached to it. But it is very familiar.

"About trows, I suppose. I don't recall. But they did say a witch was hanged and burned here."

"When would that have been?"

"I've not any idea about that." John puffed at his pipe. "A long time since. Time of the Stewarts, maybe?"

"Did the Stewarts especially dislike witches?"

"I don't know they disliked them especially."

The young man walked over to the mound, carefully for the drop was quite steep to the north. He looked down at the roof of his own cottage below.

"It was excavated not many years back," John said. "My Laurie helped the folk from the museum."

"Did they find anything?"

"Oh, it wasn't much. These mounds were all of them looted long ago. Vikings or I don't know what. But they found some old things and some jumbled Pictish bones. Old

I Have Not Answered

bones. They took the artefacts away with them. They're in storage in a basement somewhere, I doubt."

The young man knelt and placed his hand on a patch of ground. Had he the senses I have, he would have felt the roots of the heather sucking away beneath him, worms moving in the earth, the rolling of dead things.

A perplexed look came into his eyes. He rooted his fingers in the earth and came up with a jagged bit of black stone. He looked at it closely, then placed it in his pocket.

"Folk told that for a long time afterward, nothing would grow where the burning was." John looked at the heather around him. "But if ever that was true, it's not true now."

"The name. Murnin Kame. Where does it come from?"

"Well. *Murnin* means weeping, ken? That's all I can think."

"Surely, there were stories?"

"Nothing you'd call history."

"There's not much I call history."

"It was about the witch, maybe. But there's a tale about a girl who loved a trow. But knew she couldn't be with him."

"Could you tell me that one?"

"Oh, no." John laughed. "That's one of Paul's tales."

The young man smiled sweetly. "Maybe just give me the outline. You needn't actually tell the story."

"No, no, boy. That wouldn't do it justice. It was a very moving tale."

"What was the girl's name?"

"I don't know. Christie or Christine or something. Well."

It was not, in fact, a story I very much wanted to hear. Their stories of trows are so limited in scope, cannot obtain a true perspective. They are hardly worth thinking on.

The day – short though it was – was still, and Foula wore a mask of fog, shadowing the west. The island lay silent, calling no one.

"Well," said John. "It'll soon be dark."

"Yes."

They started back along the spine of the ridge.

"And how's my Laurie getting on?"

"What's that?"

"It can be difficult, for a father."

"I've heard as much."

"You've been here so long, you're practically a neighbour."

"Thank you."

"A father can't always know what's happening with his son."

"Laurie's fine."

"Yes, I should think that." John was quiet for a moment. "That with Graham and all. And May."

"And May?"

"It can be difficult to know."

The sky darkened rapidly as they came down off the hill.

"In my youth, it wasn't like this. Things were more open."

The young man bit his lip.

"You're close to May," John said.

"Not really very close."

"It's not my place to ask."

I Have Not Answered

"You haven't asked anything. It's OK."

"Well."

The sheep in the field moved aside for John. As the young came man up behind, they started and fled, bleating their discontent. Fog slid down the slopes, and the men saw it coming. They walked on, but soon the land had vanished into grey.

"Let us wait here a minute." John knocked his pipe and filled it with fresh tobacco.

Sheep sounds came through the fog, wet bleats, snuffs, grunts. I sensed them moving beyond vision, distorted and obscured. Fog is a thing that is very old. It rises from the peat, imbued with the essence of that which came before, imbued even with the dust of those who have crumbled. It has no soul yet is dead.

A flame flared up in the fog as John lit his pipe. Tobacco smoke mingled its sweetness with the hanging particulate water.

John asked, "When do you think you'll be leaving?"

"There's just one thing I need."

"Well. I wish you luck on that."

"But I've grown attached. Aberdeen seems so foreign. The traffic and cars and people. It's so busy. Here—this is a place you can discover yourself, learn about your soul."

"Aye, well. I suppose that's right enough. There's folk come just for that."

The young man peered at him closely, fog intervening. "That story. About Christie."

"It's not my place."

"It may be what I need."

"No one needs that, boy. It's just the one tale. And there's some things best left unspoken."

The young man shut his eyes. "Everything should be spoken. All is dust. There's only goodness in truth."

"Eh?"

"There's only truth in goodness."

"Well."

This obstinacy was nearly unbearable. It angered me.

The young man clenched his fists, then hid them in his jacket pockets. "John."

"Hmm?"

"I have to find out."

John fiddled with his pipe. "You'll have to speak with Graham about that."

★

ONE NIGHT while the young man slept, I heard a tremendous crash in the sky, and a wave of fire spread across the horizon. Then he was in a croft house, all in disarray, with jumbles of bones piled about, weathered and bleached. In the hearth sat a little man, red as blood, its eyes clotted and dark. But in the middle of its brow burned an eye of fire, blazing the room in light, as if it were a universal conflagration and not just the smouldering little dot of an eye. This little man, it was like

I Have Not Answered

an angel of the one whose name may not be spoken, yet it became – through some crazed distortion – as the dribble of seed that follows the procreative exertions of the Earth. In its hands, it held a thing very like a long thin polished blade. The blade was streaked with blood. I looked up and saw that the little man was not blood red in the slightest but burned, rather, with a morbid phosphorescence, like that thrown up by rotting whales that have drowned themselves upon the beach. The eye in the middle of its brow emitted a ray of sick green light as if to drown the world. And I noticed that it was not at all a knife it held in its hands but rather a harp and a cup. The young man reached for the harp and played. It was a song of sorrow. He reached for the cup and drank.

And then he was in a profound dull tunnel, and a monotonous piping was in me, then a rushing of air, which broke the horns of cattle in the hills. The young man held in his hand a long thin blade, tarnished by centuries but gleaming still. Smeared across it were the passions of men, whose dreams are strange, whose desires are strange, who know nothing save death and birth, cavernous in their longings.

Had I held that knife in my hand, I would have killed someone and spilled it.

Yet it was only the young man in the tunnel.

I woke with a start and looked over at the young man.

He slept peacefully in bed.

I went over to see if, indeed, it was true that he had not been dreaming and that this vision had been something else, had come from a source within me.

As I approached, he opened his eyes and began to dream, waking yet asleep. Through his dream eyes, I saw a figure approach as he lay in bed. Somehow I sensed he could not move. I felt as though I should recognise this figure but could not. She wore her nightshirt with the top two buttons undone.

She stooped.

And lingered.

And with her lips unravelled time, that he might for a moment be unfurled—the thought of a thought, which passes, so that only thought remains, a blotch of darkness where light had been.

My fingertips were set to explode. I felt her lips upon me, searching, drawing out a truth from the core of my being, which breaks, unmissed.

That you might have seen it when the world began. Time in revolution, unlevelled, awakened. And her lips were like the soothing of a burn that rises from the deep peat. Her smell was of mixed spring blossoms, honey, and thyme.

If you could have seen it.

All past in an instant.

A bitter agony, that. Yet once complete, perfect in its exculpation.

He woke in darkness.

There was silence through the door and window.

I Have Not Answered

"May," he whispered, in hope and fear.

I looked about but sensed no uncanny presence in the room.

He sat up in bed, afraid, and reached under the blanket, only to pull his hand away in disgust.

The young man cleaned himself in the bathroom, where a bottle of opaque lilac glass sat on the shelf. Though he was not as thin as he had been on the night Graham had gone to sea, he was nonetheless still very thin. For a moment, I could have sworn that I saw through him, through to the sink and the wall behind. He walked back out into the main room.

"May." He sobbed. "You had faith."

Of a sudden, weakness came over me, and I needed to sit.

"You didn't mean to. No. You couldn't help it. Your hands were loath and cold. You weren't in control."

He sat on the edge of the bed, pale, naked.

"You wouldn't hurt her. You love her and belong to her. Isn't it enough to love? You're dust. You're a stage in the cycle. You travel the path to awakening."

Yet the words fell dull and lifeless from his lips.

The young man began to weep. It was heartrendingly melancholic to hear.

"Sal..."

★

GRAHAM STOOD by the sink, a glass of whisky in his hand. The young man leaned on the countertop, watching.

"John told me a story," the young man said.

"Did he that?"

"About how Murnin Kame got its name."

Graham drank. "Another of dy redemption tales?"

"It's not my tale. It's yours."

"I dunna have any tales. Told dee that already, boy."

"Is there a girl in it? Named Christie?"

"Names. Names dunna matter."

"Names matter to me."

"They're just a thing du gets when du's born."

"Is it a redemption tale, then?"

"Ach, boy. What makes dee think I kens this story?"

"John said."

"And du's trusting a storyteller to tell the truth?"

I have stood at the extremity of Eshaness and looked down into the waters. Sometimes, the spray comes up over the cliffs. There are holes dug deep in the rock by the ancient pounding of the ocean, which courses the Earth like blood. And there, in storm, I can feel myself possessed of the world.

I have no great power. The plants and people and beasts have grown and withered all around me. Yet I remain. I have tasted the sea rising above the cliffs, and I have let the simmer dim filter through me as through a pane of frosted glass. Each place I set foot is no better or no worse for it. They have called me, in their ignorance, God of the Fertile Dew, and they have called me God of Destruction. But no. I am contiguous with the world, neither the one nor other.

I Have Not Answered

Everywhere I look, I am there. And everywhere is as empty as myself. Whatever they call me, I will not answer.

The young man asked, "Has it to do with the sea?"

"Is that what du thinks? That all my problems can be explained by stories about trows and such?"

"It's not about you."

"And they say I'm the crazy one."

"I don't say you're crazy."

"Du wouldna tell a madman he was crazy. Du'd sit by and let him go mad and ask him for stories."

If you go far enough north, you will come to an island called Muckle Flugga. They say that north of this island, there is no land at all until such a time as the word *north* ceases to have meaning. But before you reach this time, there is meant to be a place where there is ice all year round. And even there, things are living. Seals and bears and whales and things. The whales get trapped in the ice sometimes so that even they cannot escape. It is the way of nature. It is the key.

The young man said, "You saw something that night."

"I've telled dee what I saw. And I kens it's no right."

"What happened?"

"What happened is, du came here."

"Before."

"Things was fine before."

"No. You were a useless unemployed alcoholic then too."

Graham slammed his glass onto the counter. "Du wants my story? Should I have some tale about how I married too young, and the fishing went, and the fish farming killed my back, and the money was never enough, and there's always drink if a man just wishes it, and I've a daughter what canna sort herself out? And how I see things as canna be but how they come true all the same? And so du can write it all down in dy little notebook as some story about trows and selkies and Foula? What makes dee think there's an explanation? That the one thing's connected to the other? I'm no my father, and I'm no a teller of tales. I'm just a man what's ruined his life. There's no deeper meaning. That's dy story."

Their passions are such as I cannot fathom. They are deeper even than the Cole Deep, at the bottom of which lie things that swallow you whole and believe they do so to honour those who came before. In this, they are mistaken. Whether they were insane from the beginning or whether it is their impotent devouring that has made them so, I do not know.

"I know it's not all simple," the young man said. "There are things I can't explain. That's why I have to know."

Graham had calmed somewhat. "Stories just happen."

"I'm not talking about stories. I mean—that night. You were there. And I was too. Why? Why should either us be there? Why did you come to the beach that first day with the seal? Intuition? Fine. But look. That night. I could swear I heard a voice. A voice told me to go to the beach."

Graham poured himself a drink. "We all hear things, boy."

"There are things. And then there are *things*. There are times I can *see* it. Not all the time. But sometimes. It stands in the corner, watching me, following my every move. And if you saw it yourself. You'd know."

"Is du saying du thinks the selkies was true?"

"No. Or maybe. But they represent something. And the fact it's just in our heads: That's a kind of truth too, isn't it?"

"That's no the kind of truth a man can live by."

This Graham Stevens is monstrous. He denies the truth he cannot see and despises the truth he can. Lying is not observed among the irregularities of my kind, so I know what I say is true. Since the beginning, he has stood in the young man's way. There is a truth the young man cannot reach because of him. If the young man had not been standing there, I do not know what I might have done, what punishment would have been proportionate to this animal's endless crimes.

"But it's the only truth we have," the young man said with some menace. "Have you seen them?"

Graham was furious now. "I've seen nought. Can du no understand? There's no redemption. We each live the life we deserve. We do it to wirselves. And if du's no happy with dy own life, it'll no be solved by a tale that I'm pained to tell dee."

"Was there a harp?" the young man asked.

"To hell with dy harps."

"A cup?"

Graham picked up the bottle of whisky and threw it so hard against the wall that it shattered on the plastered and papered stone. "Whatever du wants of me, it's no a thing I can give." Graham began walking out.

"I care," the young man said to Graham's back.

"I've little enough life of my own," Graham called out over his shoulder, "to waste it on dy cares."

The young man passed the rest of the evening drinking.

When it had got quite late, he looked at the kitchen floor. Shards of glass lay scattered across it, sickening in the drying whisky. The young man fetched the dustpan and brush and set himself to the task. But the whisky was already sticky, so he wet some paper towels and began going about it that way.

He cut a finger on the glass.

He stared as his blood dripped onto the floor.

A tiny sea of blood formed, specked by islands of glass.

And he kept staring, mesmerised, until the bleeding stopped of its own accord. The light in the room had turned hazy and unreal.

A thought seemed to come to him. He retrieved the torch from the cupboard and walked to the northeast corner of the main room, by the front door. Bending down, he took hold of the corner of the linoleum, and pulled. It had been there many years and did not budge. Taking a jagged black stone from his pocket, he used it to work the corner sufficiently away from the wall for him to peel it back. Beneath the linoleum lay a sort of trapdoor. Seeing that this too had been sealed by the passage of feet and time, he gouged at the edges until the door was loose enough to lift by its ring.

Must and foulness came up from the chamber. The space below was covered in mud, but the outlines of rough flagging

I Have Not Answered

were just about visible beneath. The young man lowered himself into the hole. The walls were smeared with mud all the way up to the low ceiling.

He shined the torch in front of him. I suppose he expected to find a skeleton. I certainly expected to find a skeleton.

But the torch illuminated nothing.

It did not even illuminate a fourth wall. Before him was darkness. He advanced crouching into the black. As he went, the ceiling became higher, and the mud gradually thinned, then disappeared entirely, until at last the walls, floor, and ceiling were all of stone, hewn out in ages past by some titanic or remorseless force.

How far we walked down that dead corridor, I do not know. It was as in a dream. But at last, something faint glowed before us, and we hastened toward it. It was a little chamber, hexagonal in shape, in which a figure sat.

I had thought before that the tunnel walls were black, but this was not the case, for when compared with this figure, the stone seemed not to exist at all. Its skin and eyes were gold, and from its wrinkled pate sprouted bent wiry hair, like the mangled strings of some broken harp. In this little man, I felt a pang of recognition, as if viewing a familiarity in an ancient mirror or through a pane of frosted glass. Yet it was by some cursed distortion changed into a thing utterly strange. Although it did not move, I could sense it once had lived.

As the young man approached, I saw it was holding a thing in its hands very like a golden chalice brimming with blood.

The young man lifted the chalice to his lips and drank. Blood coursed through him as though he were a dead thing come alive. He closed his eyes and screamed, and I closed mine for the horror of it.

I woke from the dream with a sensation of cold wetness around my legs. At first, I thought it was the blood, but when I opened my eyes, I found that I stood knee-deep in the sea. The young man stood beside me, his eyes glassy and wide with horror, fixed on the monstrous island to the southwest.

Then he woke. He came to himself, looked down at the water, then up at the beach. He was trembling – shaking, I guess, from the cold – as he sloshed back onto the dry shingle.

He did not have on his jacket, so it made sense he was cold. With a glance back toward Foula, he started for home.

★

THERE IS A THING they have in town on the last Tuesday of every January called *Up-Helly-Aa*. It is not a very old thing, but they are quite fond of it.

Up-Helly-Aa is somewhat similar to their other festivals like Christmas and Bonfire Night and the things they did before their god reached these shores. On Up-Helly-Aa, their men dress in costumes and burn a boat, which is quite special, I understand. Not so much the costumes as the part about the boat. There are some of them who dress as Northmen, for that is a favourite pretence of theirs. Yet most of these

I Have Not Answered

men in costumes – called *guizers* – dress as other things, and they do so in squads, so that there are whole flocks of them. After they have burned their boat, they go around in their squads and put on plays and dances for people in various halls around town. It is a thing from which they gain much enjoyment. There are tourists who come too, just to see the Northmen and the boat.

May and the young man drove to town in the afternoon. It was winter, but there were many people in the Street, even during the day, for the shops were all open, and the tourists had little else to do but buy souvenirs. It is not like in the summer when they can go and look at puffins and things.

There was an expectancy in the air, as if something truly unique were about to take place. Though, as I say, it happens every year, without fail. But their lives are so short, a year seems to them a very long time. The squad of Northmen goes around town during the day, and people take photographs. Even the young man took some photographs. Not too many though. He told May he did not wish to look like a tourist.

To observe the procession, the young man and May positioned themselves on Upper Hillhead, among the crowd of onlookers. About a thousand men were gathered on the street in their squads. Some dressed as soldiers, others as fish, yet others as Scotsmen. And many more dressed as women. Or rather, as people resembling women, for they wore bright clothes and had plastic breasts sticking out from their shirts, which, in my experience, is not a thing that actual women often do. Each of these guizers held a large stick, swaddled in something at the top.

Seeing all this humanity below and alongside me, I almost for a moment felt something like pity for them. They seem most happy when they are dressed up, pretending to be something they are not. It must be a very tiresome life, lying all the time. They are like the things in Deepdale. The women will dress as men and the men as women, all in masks. But nothing ever changes in its essentials.

The guizers chatted and drank among themselves. Then the call went out, and flares came up at various points among this mass of men, casting everyone in pink light, the shadows blacker than ever. They lit their torches from the flares and lifted them onto their shoulders. The January night flashed sweltering. There was a cruelty to it, all that fire.

And I recalled the days past, the long before, when the land itself was fire, and the bodies of those who had built it lay scattered here and there, and then in mounds, mangled corpses reaching up, grasping in death after some final exculpation.

It was not forthcoming.

There stalked the land things from the nightmares of things unmentionable, and we each of us just with our long thin blades tempered in the hearths of abomination. What hope there was lay rotting among our fellows.

And yet they speak of redemption. For there is none of it left to us, who have suffered more, and more keenly, whose hollow sockets have witnessed glories left unfulfilled, and

I Have Not Answered

defiled, by our own hands, the last endeavour of which must be to worship the strife that smote us.

The Royal British Legion Pipe Band played up the street. Through the ranks of guizers marched the Northmen, their boat following behind. They were dressed in red and blue and plates of chrome and wore large beards stained with beer. Their leader stood aboard his boat, axe and shield raised victorious. Sign of war, wings of raven, blood sated.

I saw them all there before me, in days past. Their slaughter echoed ours. The people who had settled this land millennia since, slain and hacked, name of the unspeakable on their lips, with ravens floating over. And the Northern conquerors stood, content with what they had spoiled. The strongholds were fired, and they burned their witches and priests both. You will perhaps think it trivial, these actions of men. But I sensed in it a clattering back and the antic corybantic jollity of my own foes from the long before.

Once the Northmen had passed, the other squads followed, coming around from behind, their heat phenomenal. The young man leaned on the railing, observing closely, but May hung back and was eventually jostled from her place. She kept a hand on his shoulder, not wishing to be separated, I guess. He turned to her and shouted something, but it was very loud, what with all the people and the music.

I was reminded of a thing I could not place, of an intimacy eleven-twelfths forgotten, which badgers the consciousness precisely because it defies recollection.

She leaned closer, against his back, setting her ear to his mouth. But I do not suppose that what he had shouted had been very significant, for he seemed at a loss as to what to say and instead just nodded, his lips brushing her ear.

Rows and rows of torch bearers passed, grinning in their masks. They had gathered to celebrate nothing in particular. Up-Helly-Aa celebrates nothing. It is but a reflection of their way of being. Laurie was somewhere among them, in one of the squads, was one of the big ladies with plastic breasts carrying a load of peat on his back. There were even these things meant to be trows, all false noses, fake hair, brown face paint, and rags for clothes.

The galley reached the centre of the playing field a few blocks off, and the guizers trooped up around it. Their songs were sung, their torches cast, the boat conflagrating like the gaseous corpse of a beached whale, sparks flung into the night. Then fireworks flashed up, splitting the darkness all to bits.

Yet the sky remained unmoved, unchanged in its essentials.

The crowd grew less. Some went home. Others made their way to the halls, while the tourists and less devoted among them would soon fill the now-empty bars.

"What thinks du?" May asked, her hand still on the young man's shoulder even after the stance had ceased its utility.

"A grand party."

"It's wir heritage. Tourists come, but it's still wir festival."

"There's something elemental about it."

"We're closer to nature here."

"I understand."

She angled her head. "Does du really?"

"I don't know."

She reflected his smile. "Ach, Innes. Du's a sensitive soul. Too fragile for this world. It's lucky du has me to care for dee." She took his hand. "Come. We've a hall to attend."

May led the young man along the Hillhead and through the car park, which was busy with folk, all loitering about. They came upon a cluster of teenagers from Walls, and she accepted half a tin of their beer.

"To warm dee," said a teenage boy.

"It's aye warm. Has du kept it in dy pants the while?"

The teenager lifted to her his middle finger. They laughed.

But the atmosphere was uneasy, for the teenagers did not know the young man, a mysterious quantity from the outside.

May and the young man continued, descending the dark lane and coming out onto the Street right beside the Grand. Inside, they showed their tickets and received stamps on their hands, branding them as revellers. Tonight, Posers served as a hall. I do not know if it thereby ceased to serve as a nightclub, but the mood was indeed different. A band played waltzes, and the people danced as in days past. May joined her school friends — Karen, Sonya, and Jean — while the young man bought drinks for everyone. He is very well trained.

Karen looked at the young man with suspicion as he handed her a drink. May accepted with a smile. Sonya whispered something to Jean, which set Sonya off laughing.

The young man was super-aware, taking it all in, the glances, giggles, everything. He was studying them all, a god surveying his creatures. Yet there was a reticence, a kind of grimness I did not understand. Here, with a world of animals before him, specimens from which he could pick and choose at his leisure. I might not have even noticed had he not been so long under my observation, but I am sure it is quite true: His hand was often in his pocket, toying with something. It may have been something sharp, that little stone of his perhaps, for he at times winced as if in pain.

The first of the squads came in and performed a play about wind turbines. There was clapping and cheering, for most of the audience were drunk. The young man drank but little, and there were moments when his eyes met those of May. His were eyes of sorrow, yet hers were eyes of joy.

And in his hand, he held a beer glass like a chalice but was loath to drink of it.

I thought upon the marching epochs in procession and how many had been born and been dead without reason, each holding a chalice from which he might drink.

And the reek of the dead was about me, though I was surrounded by such life, so that I sensed the madness of it all, this endless waltz of existence, around and back again. Had I not been there to see it begin, at the cusp of the end of those who came before? Had I not tasted that sweet wine, which bubbles up from the deep peat, pure and unbroken, yet turns to blood in your mouth? All these animals, coursing with blood, dying to be spilled. Were they all to perish, would that be the end of blood? No, it would seep into the peat and rise again, new and ancient. A fish cannot drown in water.

The breaks between squads lessened until they flowed through the hall in a continual stream. The Northmen entered and sang their wonted songs, axes raised in conquest.

Every guizer has a duty
When he joins the festive throng.
Honour, freedom, love, and beauty
In the feast, the dance, the song.

Worthy sons of Vikings make us,
Truth be our encircling fire.
Shadowy visions backward take us
To the Sea-King's fun'ral pyre.

They were followed by the women with peat, who danced a suggestive jig, had time to swallow a dram, then bustled out. Laurie raised his mask, greeted them drunkenly, and kissed May on the cheek so as not to smear her lipstick. But the others were calling to him, and his leaving was swift.

May returned with drinks, handing one to the young man. Her words were lost in the noise, for the music was loud, but I sensed she chided him for neglecting to drink. The liquid she gave him was sweet and red. He twirled the slender black straw in the glass, and May laughed. Karen and Sonya did not notice as they were busy speaking with men at the time. Jean noticed because she was there with her boyfriend, and they were busy ignoring one another.

"What is it?" the young man asked.

"Try," said May.

He held the glass to his eyes. Bubbles rose and broke into the air. Where bubbles in fizzy drinks come from, I do not know. But they appear to come from the bottom of the glass.

May moved in closer, was right up against him. "Try."

"Sometimes, I feel as though I'm—"

"Will du no drink already?" May eased the glass from his hands and took a sip. "See? Safe."

"I feel as though I'm going mad."

"Yeah, du's mad alright. But du's no so much a man as du canna try a girlie drink, is dee?"

"Things happen at night."

May pressed herself to him, gazing into his eyes. "They do. An awful lot of bairns is born in Shetland in October."

The young man looked past her, squeezing the sharpness in his pocket.

"Nine months after Up-Helly-Aa, ken?"

"I... Imagine things about you."

"Hmm... What is it du imagines?"

"You don't understand."

"Men are animals."

They are pointless and unpredictable. They breed, are slaughtered, then breed again. It is their nature. They cannot help but be what they are. In all of nature, nowhere is transcendence possible, least of all for them. At the last revolution, they shall be dust forever.

She raised the red drink to his lips. "Try."

"I'm afraid."

"Du's no need to fear me, Innes. I was afraid. But I'd no reason to be. I realise that now."

He closed his eyes. "If I for one moment let go, I might never wake again."

She stroked his face. "Then let me sleep beside dee."

He drank.

A warmth came through me, like the coursing of blood. Images entered my dream eyes, or his, I do not know, for no one was dreaming. There was a girl, her hair long, black, shining. Her smile was as the moon drowned in the sea. She would have been the most beautiful thing alive, were she yet living. On the ground beside her rested an empty chalice and a harp of gold.

The young man's thin body shuddered, and languid though May was, she kept a steadying arm around his waist.

"Du's drunk."

"I've seen things." He shook his head. "I've touched things."

She was dreaming yet awake.

"I keep them in a box under my bed."

"Du's no making any sense." She drank from his glass, then raised the sweet red fluid to his lips again. "Have more."

"I'm dizzy."

"Let's go." She took another sip, then offered him the glass one last time, and now he accepted in earnest, draining its contents. Without saying goodbye to her friends, she took his arm and led him from the club, from the hotel, into the night.

People were roaming. Some had come out of bars, but others were hall-goers who had tired of the amusements. Talk was everywhere, echoing off the cobblestones and masonry. A couple kissed messily in the lane, like animals. But no. This is not true. Other animals do not kiss. Only humans kiss. It is part of possessing, to take a thing in your mouth and taste it. They are cannibals, every one of them, though they are generally too weak to follow kissing to its logical conclusion.

But I have seen blood as you could not conceive. And when she played the harp, it was a sublimity like no other, such as could make the drowned moon rise.

May and the young man headed north along the Street and went down Burns Walk.

Then the sea was before them, beyond the harbour, Bressay humping up cold across the sound. There were animals here too, the inebriated discharge of Thule Bar and Captain Flint's, stumbling in groups of twos and threes and fours, carnality incarnate, the mockery of all endeavour. But they were fewer than on the Street.

"That island's Bressay," May pointed out, needlessly.

"I love you."

May looked at him, her eyes wide as those of a cow seal. "I'll hear dee say it again, for the pleasure of it."

I Have Not Answered

He squeezed hard in his pocket, and when he removed his hand, I could see it bled. "I love you."

May saw the blood, lifted his hand to her lips, and kissed it.

I too once bled, and my wounds too were kissed.

But that is all in the past, and in truth, I do not recall it.

There were tears in his eyes. "But I can't. You don't know."

She smiled.

"The things, May. I don't know me."

"Then at least there's one of wis. I kens dee. I kens du's no as du seems. Du acts so haughty and superior, but du isna. Dy soul's just too big for dee to express. And that part of dee that hurts: It's a thing I can make better."

He bit his lip.

"And du'll knit me a shawl to wear when I go out, and everywhere I am, du'll be there with me, about my shoulders."

"I can't knit."

"Du can learn."

"I don't know where I'm going."

"I kens a place."

She led him to where the Esplanade meets the Street to the south and brought him among the Lodberries, old buildings close and intimate on all sides. They came out onto the Knab, rounding the headland along the cliffs, where grass gives way to empty space and boulders at the base testify to the creeping death of the land.

When at last they reached the Sletts, she brought him down upon the rocks, cliffs rising at their backs.

And she took him there along the coast, then into the cliff, where the east winds battered somewhat less, and gave him her lips to taste.

I took from it such joy, for his sake, that I wished I were dust. I imagined how those lips tasted and even imagined I tasted them myself. I almost nearly thought for this one instant that I possessed a soul.

She brought his hands down around her and sighed when he released himself from that uncanny presence that oppressed him and kissed her back naturally, unmechanically. He cupped his hand around a buttock. She did not crumble from him but came in tighter and shone upon him softly, like moonlight through the water.

They undid themselves there, against the rock. And with their bodies, they unfurled time, the confluence of the flux, which comes and passes, a pool of light emboldening the limitless dark, like waves lapping gently against a bloated whale corpse on the beach.

There, on the Sletts, I witnessed the world's end, creation's climax, the place bubbles wake, break, and are liberated into air. It was beautiful. You would not believe it if I told you.

★

THEY BUILT A LIGHTHOUSE on Bressay many years ago, and still it casts out over the ocean, failing in the distance, where the great ships move. You can see its blink from the Sletts.

These blinks mean something, I believe. They are a kind of language I do not understand.

May and the young man sat together on the rocks, looking out across the sound. It was cold and getting colder. They huddled close, hands together.

An odd calm possessed me, as if a weight had been lifted from the soul I did not possess. My limbs were slack and numb.

She arched her back, scrabbled farther along the rocks, and laid her head in his lap. She looked up at him and smiled. Staring at the blinking light, he stroked her hair and cheek. I think his eyes may have been sad, but it was hard to tell.

She yawned, then shivered. "Is du no cold?"

"No."

"I'm cold."

He looked down at her. "I don't feel anything. I'm numb."

She closed her eyes, and her smile widened. "That's how it is, yeah? Just this feeling of..."

"Of being somewhere else."

"Yeah. Somewhere there's no one else. And we're on these rocks together, and it's just wis."

"Is it?"

"It is."

"I used to understand."

"But now?"

"But now."

She nestled her cheek into his jacket. "We'll need a place to sleep. I'll ring Jean."

Voices came down all the way from South Road, where people were trooping back to their houses in Sound after the night's festivities. There were shouts and snatches of song.

"That night," she said. "My birthday. Du sang 'Barbara Allen'. That's when I first kenned it."

"Did I sing that? I don't recall."

She hesitated. "Does du...?"

"Her name's Sal. Was Sal. I don't know."

"And what's she like, then, this Sal?"

"I don't know anymore. It's been so long. I'm someone else now."

"I've been someone else all my life."

"How's that?"

"It's just, what's the point? If du doesna have a goal, ken?"

"Everyone has a goal." he said, tracing her eyebrows with a finger. "They just don't necessarily know what the goal is."

"Kiss me."

But the position was awkward, and he could not do it.

So she shifted, and he stood and helped her. And they kissed.

When they were done, she asked, "What's dy goal?"

"I need to find a story."

"Has du no found out yet?"

"I don't think I ever will."

"Then du'll always have a goal. That's no such a bad thing."

"I need to know how it ends."

"Can du no make dy ain ending?"

I Have Not Answered

"I can make my own ending," he said. He repeated it like a prayer. "I can make my own ending."

The young man kissed her again, holding the back of her head and neck in his hands as though drinking from a chalice. But however deep he drank, he could never empty the cup.

After a while, she pulled away. "I'm cold." She took out her phone. "Jean? Du's hame? Haes du a spot we can sleep da nicht? Yeah. Sofa's braa. OK." She put the phone back in her pocket. "She's on Haldane Burgess Crescent."

They came up off the Sletts by the traffic circle, and town was before them, with its voices and people and madness.

"I can hardly bear it," she said. "After being alone."

He nodded, half aware.

"Let's go round by Westerloch instead, yeah?"

The route was ridiculously out of the way, and there was really no excuse for it on a cold night. But they went on past the traffic circle anyway. Cars occasionally swept by, in and out of town, drunks picking up drunks.

Clickimin Broch was in their eyes, lit by golden floodlights. It is a ruin now, but I remember when it yet was new, rising from the lake, a tower into the sky built by a people whose gods were close at hand. They made sacrifice and called out the ancient names.

Turning the lake, May and the young man started up into the quiet of Westerloch, then onto the walking path that completes the circuit around the lake, connecting back with Scalloway Road by the sea. Wind rippled upon the waters.

It was a light wind, and hushed. Staney Hill steeped above them to the west, and I heard voices they could not, coming from out its hollows. But there were also voices they could hear, drifting over across the loch. Disbanded guizers, perhaps. Fish, windmills, or women with their breasts out.

When May heard the voices, she paused, uncertain. The young man held and kissed her, and if she felt trapped, she did not show it. They proceeded until they came into the leisure centre car park and crossed over onto Lochside. Haldane Burgess Crescent was close now, as were the voices.

But May was resolute, and she led on, holding his hand.

★

I HAVE SEEN SUNRISE from the top of Ronas Hill. Not often, for it is far from my own place, but over the ages, the times add up to a significant number. From the hilltop, you can look out over nearly all the world. There is Northmavine asleep below, still in shadow, and across to Sullom and the rim of Yell. And so on to the first shining of Fetlar in the east.

Tourists say this is a barren country.

But it is not. There are lichen, grasses, birds, ponies, people everywhere. And there are those who are alone. I cannot recall if it was always thus. Were there others who I have forgotten? Do I know the sightless things I pass in the night? Do they know me? But it is not so. They are dust, the all of them, if ever they existed. In the end, there is only me.

I Have Not Answered

Atop Ronas Hill sits a cairn. They have removed things from it and put new things in their place. Beer cans and cigarette butts, for instance. But it is ever the same cairn, unchangeable in its essential state. They entombed people there once, carried corpses up the hill and shut them in.

I was indifferent to their gods.

Some even worshipped those among us. First they feared us, then they worshipped us. And when they had worshipped us enough, they forgot they had ever feared us, until at last they forgot we were meant to be gods. So we dwindled for them, and failed. But we had not changed; the world had changed around us.

And so too with beer cans. They are brought up on the North Boat, filled with beer. Most of them go back down on the North Boat, empty. But some stay in the lanes, on the verges, or in the cairn atop Ronas Hill. It is said that beer cans last forever. But then, there are so many things that are said, and I somehow doubt it. I am content to wait and see.

The young man did not come home until Thursday. He and May had spent the preceding day locked away in Jean's house. It was OK with Jean. She understood, for she had a boyfriend herself. When Laurie called on the mobile, May had said nothing in particular. It had been a nice night. She was staying on in Lerwick a day or two. The dance by the women with the breasts and peat had been fantastic.

So it was first on Thursday afternoon that the young man and May drove back to the Westside and that the young man went down to the beach. The mild day was all damped and fogged in so that, had he not walked the path so many times before, I think he would not have known it. But he crested the field and came down onto the shingle. The tide, invisible beyond the fog, sounded dully in the atmosphere, the terminal gurgle of little stones, the old things, being sucked away and replaced by the new.

The young man followed the rim of the beach until he came to the place of shelter he shared with Graham, beneath the overhanging wall of pebble and clay.

You would have needed to have been very observant to know it from other spots on the beach. But the young man is very observant. And there were, I suppose, certain stones he recognised. And the shingle beneath, though not *ordered* in any sense of the word, was perhaps differently chaotic than elsewhere, from so much time spent standing and shuffling there. So many stony nests built for whisky bottles—full, three-quarters, half-empty, "We may as well make good on it, boy," empty.

For it was here two men often stood – one older, one younger, panting toward their deaths with that human inevitability to which my kind cannot aspire – and drank and smoked and sometimes even said things. I know what the young man wanted from it. He wanted a story. It was a story he already knew. What Graham wanted, I would not hazard to guess. He never interested me sufficiently to prompt inquiry into his psychology.

I Have Not Answered

As for me, I desire nothing. I have never desired a thing.

The stench of the rotting seal somewhere down in the fog had long been nearly quenched by the thoroughness of decay. And besides, you would not necessarily have expected to smell it from under the overhang, for there was no wind. But in this, you would be mistaken, for the little bits of smell are taken up by the little bits of water composing the fog, and those bits of water swarm by forces best known to themselves. It may appear that the fog is quite still, but it is always moving.

I detected in the fog a hint of rot, the rot of the freshly dead. Subtle though the hint was, I believe the young man marked it the very same instant, for I was looking at him, and his eyes narrowed to slits before widening again, first to a normal degree, then to something greater, and finally back to normal again. He peered into the fog, in the direction of the seal.

He walked slowly through the fog, wishing, I think, to avoid tripping over the seal.

He saw nothing until his boot pushed up against the corpse. The reverberation of it against the tip of his boot, the echoing of this resistance up through the muscles in his leg, must have felt more solid than he would have expected from the seal's withered remains.

But the young man did not look down. He stood there, ever so still, looking out at the whiteness before him. If he had words, he did not say them, and I wished he had been dreaming, so that I could know what pictures he had. And out of pity too, maybe, to spare him the agony of wakefulness.

There came a tear into one eye, then another. Very little tears, droplets scarcely larger than that they might have joined their brethren among the fog.

And the word the young man said, softly and without distinction, was "May." It might have been a kind of prayer, though I do not know to whom.

He took a step back, then lowered to his knees, shingle crunching beneath him. At last, he looked upon the corpse, which lay directly before the bones and skin of the seal.

The young man stroked Graham's hair, as if he were a favourite cat and merely sleeping. The birds had taken his eyes, which they say are the most nutritious part, so it is not within my power to report whether they were glassy or otherwise.

New tears were in the young man's eyes, larger now, and he looked to where Graham's chest was stained with old blood. Grasped in Graham's hand was a long-bladed knife, such as you might find under a rock embedded in the hillside. The young man looked back to his face, which was just a dead animal thing, and he bent down and kissed its stubbled cheek.

Very subtly, so I did not even realise it was happening until it had already happened, the young man drew out his knees and sat with his back straight and his legs crossed. Nor had I been looking for this movement since he had not sat this way since having saved Graham from the sea. Because of the boots, it would have been impossible to place his feet upon his thighs, so he did not even try. His eyes were still open, but the fog was before them, so they might as well have been shut.

I Have Not Answered

The young man remained like this, very still, for the space of some minutes.

A vision spread out before me. The grass was around on all sides, a different texture and shade than in Shetland. It was level with the young man's dream eyes. Clinging to the tip of each blade of grass was a single drop of water.

There was a clarity to it, as though the whole world were illuminated by a directionless light, and each drop of water reflected a thousand gods, ten thousand blessed beings, a hundred thousand instructors of the path to light, a million pupils who sought this light, and much else besides. But a fresh wind brisked the droplets off the grass, into the air, and when the young man looked up, cranes were flying on a course of their own choosing. Away before us lay a mountain, with trees on its lower slopes and then a waste of snow and ice at its peak. It was to this mountain the young man travelled, not with the cranes, but of them, so that the trees and their blossoms and leaves spread out below, each detail so finely defined that I could not see the whole for its parts.

Atop the mountain, in a snowy recess, stood a building of wood, its roof sharp and spined. The building had once been painted red and gold but was now faded, disintegration imposing upon the air. All around, and in places half or fully buried in the snow, was arrayed an army of little stone statues, each perhaps a foot and a half in height. Some were of hideous creatures, demons of a sort, but many were quite like the young man's little man of jade, only larger, standing rather than sitting, and with bare bald heads. All the demons wore on their maws the same gaping silent roar, and all the men wore on their faces the same knowing smile, as though they were pleased, ever so pleased, with what they had done.

The young man ascended the steps to the building. Hoops of bells jangled from the roof as he walked beneath. He crossed the threshold and faced a darkened hall, with the mountain and the snow opening out behind. Perfumed smoke burdened the air, from the burning of exotic woods in great metal trays. Yet it could not quite dispel the stench of disintegration. In the centre of the hall squatted a great fierce man, his skin rough, hairy, blue. By his side lay a studded iron club. Curled black hair fell freely over his bared chest. This man had been looking down, working away at something, but when he looked up, enormous cutting teeth projected from his huge, bloody grin. In his clawed hands, he held the head of a man, its face chewed away.

The blue man raised himself. His language was strange, yet I somehow understood. "Would you deny me my meal?"

The young man asked, "Why must you take the flesh alone?"

"All is flux. All changes, renewed. The spirit is beyond me."

"Why must the spirit continue? Where will it end?"

But the blue man said nothing. He resumed his meal.

I wished that the young man's dream eyes, or whatever they were, would turn from the scene, for disgust rose within me, yet he watched, unmoved. Flesh was torn from the head, and soon the blue man was polishing and licking a bare skull.

I HAVE NOT ANSWERED

The vision vanished.

Yet still the young man was not alone. There stood behind him a woman dressed in a tattered green jacket. Such was the abruptness of the vision's end, it took me an instant to realise it was May. Her hand was on the young man's shoulder.

There was a light wind, and the fog had cleared. I had been lost for some time in the young man's reverie.

He remained sitting, but the peace was gone from him, and he trembled. "I loved him," he said.

"I know," said May. Her eyes were full of sorrow, but I am not sure for whom. She took a moment before continuing. "At least now, he's at peace."

The young man said nothing.

★

IN THE DAYS that followed, Laurie stayed close by, troubled though he was. I do not know that he ever mentioned it, what had happened. Not in my hearing at least. But he must have known. Jean's boyfriend would have told him, or word would have slipped out from someone with the police. They are like that, men. They tell each other things.

And I suppose I felt sorry for the young man. He had not got his story. I do not care about the story one way or another, but for his sake, it was unfortunate. And then, he had told May he had loved him. Though I do not believe it. This had been a harmless exaggeration, said to sooth her. Graham

Stevens had been an animal, undeserving of his love. No, he was less than that even, for animals do not destroy themselves.

The young man began again to sit on the floor with his legs crossed and burn his scent cones. Though he did not stop eating and drinking this time, nor keep himself locked inside. He continued life in a way.

I guess May was sad. I think I saw her crying at the house once. But some women are good at hiding it. The young man would come by to be comforting or something, but Laurie was always around, and there was a certain tension. And also when Laurie and May copulated on the sofa at his house, like animals, she could have been crying, which is a queer thing. Most animals experience pleasure from copulation.

Yet they all turned out when they buried him. They did not take him into a cairn at the top of a hill. They do not do that anymore, not even with very important people, like folk who have been on the Council. Just a space of earth with the sea beside. The young man said something about seals being able to watch the grave. I do not know whether the others heard, but May did. I think maybe she cried then too.

Laurie put his arm around her to bring comfort, and she turned her face away so no one could see.

★

WHILE THE YOUNG MAN slept, the door to the cottage opened, and a figure walked in, seating itself on the edge of the bed.

I HAVE NOT ANSWERED

The young man seemed to wake, but somehow I sensed he could not move.

"I am in the deep Earth," Graham Stevens said. "There are tunnels deep into the world. At the end of every one lie those who came before. The dead dance around them to the monotonous beating of a drum and tuneless mad pipings. I would dance with them, but I cannot, for my limbs are loath and cold. There is a harp for me to play there, yet from its strings I can draw nothing but an insane hum that would lull the very stars to sleep. So I play, and the stars sleep, and the great masses sleep before me while the dead dance all around."

The young man managed to shut his eyes, and my vision vanished. When he opened them again, May was sitting on the edge of the bed. She was, in the moonlight, so lovely and pale and still. She leaned down and kissed him, her lips damp and chill. I could nearly feel them myself. He reached out from beneath the blanket and placed a hand on the side of her head, which was wet from the rain, brushing the pale skin of her cheek. A terror came upon him, and he drew back. Wondering, I looked more closely.

And I saw.

Her eyes were like frosted glass, and crawling things moved beneath her skin, burrowing through the rot. A stench like that of a dead seal filled the room.

He woke with a scream.

May woke too and moved up against him, though since the bed in the cottage was so narrow, they were already very close. He turned his head and looked at her moonlit face, searching for something he could recognise. But I think, in this mood of his, he found everything strange. It was like when he looked at the things in the box beneath the bed.

"May..."

She threaded her hand through his.

"I'm scared," he said.

"We're all scared."

"I never know whether it's real or not."

"It's real."

He shut his eyes for a moment, then opened them.

All was as it had been.

"There's so much I don't understand."

He need not be scared. I am with him. May is fickle, untrustworthy. Animals play with things, then tire of them. But I am otherwise. I will protect him. I will never leave him.

"Du thinks too much."

A moment later, she was asleep.

He stared at the ceiling, following its cracks. They were cracks of time, created by the settling of things. If the cottage remains standing another fifty years, and I do not think it will, the cracks then will be entirely different, following the lines that have already been set yet branching out mysteriously.

There are none who can predict the settling of the Earth. Even I, who have been so long, cannot do that.

The young man was whispering to himself, and I came in very very close to hear. His breath played hot and moist on my ear. "They lead each to those who came before. Every crack is a life that has come and passed. You see houses the country across, life within and life without. Ponies bearing baskets of peat, the living dead earth bared over by however many tushkars, cutting away, casting off. You see cracks within the Earth, travelling down to the hearts of the springs."

From her breathing, I could tell that May had woken and was listening. But so soft were his words, she surely could not discern them. The cadence, perhaps, but not the words.

"They will rise, make everything new. Awakened. Powerless now, but burgeoning. Growth flung up by a dying world."

"Innes."

The young man stopped.

"It's no easy for anyone. Du canna take all the sadness dysel."

"There's Laurie."

She did not open her eyes. "Does du care, even?"

"I care."

For the space of around two minutes, neither of them spoke.

"I never kens with dee. Du's so strange. There's times I think du cares for nothing at all, du's so tied up."

"I try to care," he said. "Sometimes my feelings are so strange. You wouldn't believe it if I told you."

"No." She sounded sad.

The young man put his hand on her cheek, but she turned away and rolled over.

★

THE YOUNG MAN passed the next days looking through his notes. He sought to piece his story together from fragments here and there. Murnin Kame, a girl named Christie, a cup and a harp. Universal motifs. But how did the story end? The Middle English *Sir Orfeo* poem ends happily, with the human escaping the fairies. So too the 'King Orfeo', 'Hind Etin', 'Tam Lin', and 'Power of the Harp' ballads. But not 'Elf-Shot', 'Little Kersti', and 'Agnete and the Merman'. Did a tragic Norse ending migrate into Britain via Shetland, thereby informing later interpretations of the Classical Orpheus story?

I do not understand the half of this, but such was the state of his notes. He would stare at the photos he had taken of Graham and put on the computer, looking for a kind of truth.

He went and re-interviewed Henry from Norby, Ron Seatton, all he could reach. But as little as they would talk about the story before, they were even less willing now. They said among themselves it was polite "not to speak ill of the dead." This is a fear they have. Names are a strange thing. If you know a thing's name, you might gain power over it. But equally, if you speak its name, it might gain power over you. It is best neither to ask nor respond, to call nor answer. Give away as little as you can. The less a thing knows about how much you know, the better.

And so it is with people. They know this internally, even if the reasons have long been forgotten. Graham Stevens is beyond harm, their inner voices tell them. But could it be that he might still have the power to harm us? Do we call his spirit to us when we speak of him? And might he not thus grasp hold of our minds and seek to drag us into his world?

I say this as they think it, enshrouded by their superstitions.

The young man did not learn what he wanted. And so he stood one night, shivering in his coat, on the shore.

He spoke, whether to himself or to the dead stars, I cannot say. "He never told you his story. He was afraid of his truth, couldn't face reality, and it killed him. You could've helped him make his own ending. You could've unburdened him, moved him toward the light. But you were powerless."

I bridled at this resignation, this expression of impotence.

He ceased shivering, and a change came over his face. "You need the story. You have the power. You can make your own ending. You've a power that you haven't used. You've kept your blade hidden. You'll bend them to your will.

"And if that passion might be fulfilled, the Earth's longing, deeper than the longings of men alone. The entirety of creation at your fingertips, buzzing, cycling with existence, through the before and the after, smiting time with the perspective of eternity. Value is determined in retrospect, at the end, when you can see the law as a whole, when the pattern is complete or when you're capable of seeing the pattern that was complete from the start.

"Achieve your desire. Then you'll have the knowledge to help others walk their paths. But first, achieve your desire. You owe them nothing. You can't know what you owe them until you have awakened. And then your depths – deeper than theirs – will rise awfully from the peat, subjugating their base desires, your will exculpated by its ineluctability."

These words flowed into me like the loveliest of music, the secret song of the harp. Yet even as I shuddered in pleasure for it, the young man shuddered in a paroxysm of abhorrence.

And he began to cry.

There is a queer thing they keep in a glass case at the museum in town. It is a big stone that looks vaguely like a lump of fat, and you might nearly imagine it was good to eat. In reality, it is hard and dry. But also in reality, the stone is a lump of fat. It is a hunk of butter that was sunk into the peat in the Northmen's time, and in the peat, it was preserved and turned to stone. You cannot eat it, yet it retains the semblance of food. It has changed from one thing to another, yet its essential nature remains. It is impossible to say whether this thing should be called a lump of fat or a stone.

People, in their ignorance, would call it the ghost of butter. But really, I do not suppose I believe in such things myself, not in the same way. Ghosts, I have never encountered. It is a mundane human delusion to think their kind so exalted in the universe that, even after they perish, there is reason to remain. The human perspective is so limited. It is possible to take a body yet let the soul stay within it. And when such a thing is done, the body and soul together, ripped from their mundanity, can sometimes become an entirely new thing, a dark gap in existence. These gaps, they drag you in and close up behind.

I Have Not Answered

You would think the stars were dead, there is so little light.

Gradually though, in the black, you begin perceiving a faint glow, as from some putrid mouldy phosphorescence, and you find yourself in a strange dark tunnel, familiar yet apparently untravelled. You have no choice but to walk these paths – stooping at times where the ceiling drops – seeking an exit. Corridors branch off, as in a hideous rabbit warren, and you can venture epochs, so I am led to believe, in these tunnels.

And it may be that you see a brighter light ahead and think for a moment you are not so entirely closed off after all and that it is, in fact, day shining before you. Should you approach it though, you will be disappointed, for at the end of every path, you will find only yourself, and nothing is so fearful as seeing yourself through another's eyes.

There are rooms too that are all blocked up and into which you cannot enter. Yet somehow you know these chambers are there, hidden though they are behind the tunnel walls. What is locked away in these rooms, you cannot know, save that it must be of immeasurable value for someone to have gone to such efforts to conceal it. Their contents can only be sensed vaguely, as a thought that passes, never open to you, just glimpses, here and there.

And maybe in the dark, you see the face of a beautiful girl, her hair so black as to turn the walls white by compare. And if she were to play music, it would be on a harp, and if she were to drink, it would be from a golden chalice. And if the moon were to rise, it would drown in the sea.

I woke on the ridge of Murnin Kame, looking out to haughty Foula.

How I had got there and how long I had been lost in reverie, I cannot say. Did the young man still live in the cottage? Had humans perished themselves with their bombs and carbon dioxide emissions and uncooked seafood? Had the young man ever existed at all, or had the whole story been a dream I could never have? Was I now the same being I had been before waking? Or had I transformed into a new thing? I could be my own impossible dream. For all I know.

There is so much I do not remember.

★

LAURIE SAID NOTHING, did not even nod in greeting when he opened the door. His muscles tensed, however, in a manner imperceptible to those whose senses are of a lower order.

"Hi," the young man said.

Laurie stood aside.

It was dark in the house. A candle had flushed its wax, guttering out into a pool on the tabletop and locking the candlestick in place. Beside it stood a half-empty bottle of Scotch and a single grimy glass.

"I'm sorry—" the young man began.

Laurie held up a hand to stop him.

I wish I could read the workings of the young man's mind, truly become part of him as in a dream. It would be pleasant

I Have Not Answered

to know if he were really sorry or if it was just a thing he said, in the manner of men. There was a certain glint in his eye.

"I want to make things right."

Laurie crossed his arms. "You needn't bother."

"Neither of us meant for it to happen."

"That's a platitude."

"Yes."

Laurie sat on the sofa, and the young man sat beside him, maddeningly close.

"What else do you want? Other than to make things right?"

"There's something I need to know. I need the story."

"The story? You're still after the story? The story's dead, man. You killed it. Even if someone remembered, he couldn't know the story better than you."

"I'll tell you."

"Not interested. You've done enough. Graham's dead from your questions. May's—she does what she thinks best."

"Once I get the story, my work here will be done. Maybe I'll go back to Aberdeen."

"You're a monster, a demon. Only May can't see it."

The young man just stared into his eyes.

"What's your story, then?"

"There's a girl who's been with a fairy. She plays a harp the fairy's given her, and when the fairy hears it, he knows she's revealed their secret. Then maybe she escapes him, or maybe the fairy takes her away back to the hill."

"Never heard it." Laurie sounded relieved yet disappointed.

"You'd tell me, wouldn't you?"

Laurie poured whisky into the dirty glass.

The young man picked up the bottle and drank from it. "You must know something. I need to know how it ends."

"Happily."

"You're making it up."

Laurie stood. He pointed toward the door. "Get out. You can have her. I don't care."

The young man stood too, and as soon as he was standing, his strength left him. "Why? Why won't you give it to me? I need it. Why won't you give me the story?"

"I don't know the story." Laurie's face flushed red, and his fists clenched. "Du aaready kens da story, man. Du's telled it to me dyself."

"I can't have peace until I know it."

Laurie's fist shot out, punching into the young man's stomach. The young man staggered back, doubled over. He coughed, then straightened. Laurie stood poised for combat, his tall, muscular body shaking from self-restraint.

Yet the punch had changed something in the young man, so that when he looked up again, it was with an amused smile.

Laurie dropped his arms.

"I'm beyond guilt," the young man said, "I'm beyond you."

"Monster."

"You're an animal. I could never desire anything you have."

As the young man walked out, Laurie was left standing there, clenching his fists at the empty room.

I HAVE NOT ANSWERED

The sun had just enough strength left to grey the afternoon, and a curlew called from the dusk. The young man hummed cheerily as he left the house and skipped off along the track.

Somewhere, lost in my mind, a voice came to me, rich and urgent, strange but like a voice I had known before.

It was the voice of Paul Stevens. There were men and women gathered by the fire, as in days past, before the oil.

There's a girl, Paul said. *Called Christie. A bonnie peerie maid. Shining black hair down to her waist. And the bonniest blue eyes.*

'Du, Christie,' says Mother, 'why's dy shirt wet?'

'Oh, it's as I'm sweating,' says Christie.

'Sweat's clear,' Mother says.

'Oh, it's as I'm spilled a mug of ale.'

'Ale's brown. That's white.'

'Oh, it's as my breasts is full of milk.'

'And who,' says Mother, 'made dy breasts full of milk?'

'Oh, it's the king of the trows has been my sweetheart these seven years.'

Mother starts crying. And it's, 'Poor, poor Christie. Du's sold dy maidenhead too cheap.'

'Oh, no,' says Christie, 'I havena.'

'Then what's he given dee, dy trow?'

'He's given me this gold chalice. And when I'm sad, I can drink. And be happy.' *Fills that cup with ale. Takes a drink, does Christie.*

'Has du no got anything else?' says Mother.

'He's given me this gold harp. And when I'm sad, I can play. And be happy.' *Plays a sorrowful tune on that harp, does Christie.*

[195]

And before du can even think the thought, there's the king of the trows, standing afore them. 'Hold now, Christie,' says he. 'Why's du playing that harp?'

'Oh, it's as I love dee.'

'And if du loved me,' says the trow, 'du'd no be playing that harp.' And that trow.

He picks up Christie as she's a wisp of straw.

And puts her on the back of his horse. Rides up and up the Murnin Kame, up to the mound. Rides the mound three times around.

Then they's inside. She's seven sons by him, see? Seven sons by that trow. And soon as they's inside, these bairns runs up.

Laughing.

And poke and tease her.

So she's crying.

But it's 'Hush, hush. Sit dee now on this stool,' says they. And they put out a stool.

And Christie sits.

Which she shouldna have done.

'And take dee now a drink frae this cup,' says they.

Christie, she drinks frae that gold chalice. And all the time, she's thinking on Mother, on her ain people, on her Christian faith.

Her sons, they says, 'Where does du live? Where was du born? And where'd du lose dy maidenhead?'

'Oh, in Shetland I'm living and was born. And that's where I lost my maidenhead.'

'Drink again, drink again.'

She drinks again.

Which she shouldna have done.
And still, she's thinking on her ain land and people.
So her bairns, they takes that cup.
And they drops a thing in it. A grain of something.

'Drink again, drink again. Where does du live? Where was du born? And where'd du lose dy maidenhead?'

'Oh, in the mound I'm living and was born. And it's here I lost my maidenhead.'

Her peerie bairns, they laugh so hard, the whole hill shakes.
And over in the church by the voe, the crucifix falls frae the wall.
And breaks in two.
Knocks some stones from the wall, it does. On its way down.
There's a hollow in the wall.
And a body in that hollow.
A skeleton, see? Holding in its hand a key.
That skeleton's holding a key.
Key to Paradise, it was.
Back in the hill. 'What's dy sweetheart? What's dy sweetheart?'

'Oh, it's the king of the trows is my sweetheart. And I'll never leave him. Never.'

★

THE YOUNG MAN took the things out of the box one by one and placed them in a row on the bed. A hat, a bottle of perfume, a scarf, some tufts of wool, a pencil, a sock, a few bits of driftwood, a pocket notebook with some sketches, a comb with tangles of hair in it. He stared at these things, as if willing them off the bed and out of the cottage.

The wind blew loud outdoors, rushing against old stone, hitting the base of the hill, and tumbling back into the cottage's southern wall. I had seen the lights blinking in the hill as I came up the slope from the beach. It is very subtle, really. If you were inattentive, you would think you had imagined it.

He picked up the comb and held it before his eyes. It is strange that he remains interested in these items after all that has happened. Perhaps their interest stems not only from May but from something worthy of study that is essential to the items themselves.

"If it's fate, why should it be presaged? Why a pencil? Why a sock? Why these things? Only the notebook is personal."

I sensed that these thoughts had come to him long ago but had been left unsaid. And it was true, once I pondered upon it, that I had chosen odd gifts for him. If it were to study her mind, I could have taken a book on engineering. For her sex, some lace undergarments. If it were so he could gain power over her through ritual incantation, nothing would have been more useful than toenail clippings. Though as far as that goes, the hair in the comb would make a passable substitute.

He turned in my direction and looked through me to the empty armchair under the west window. "Whether you do it in some fit of madness or whether—" He cut himself off, letting a thing go unsaid. "Well, anyway." After a moment's pause, however, he began again. "It indicates a higher

I Have Not Answered

conception, a plane of your mind that's awakened to the law. What's your place in the cycle? God or a demon? But must you lose control of yourself to gain control of another? Are you the mirror, or are you what the mirror reflects? It's Foula. Foula's the call of your spirit, calling you further along the cycle toward awakening. But your worldly senses are too dull and blunt to understand the call, so you always fail to answer."

I felt uneasy, his eyes resting on the chair behind me, a grin twisted across his face. Yet I was curiously unable to move.

"But one day, your spirit will rise up and stifle your mundanity. You'll be as a god stalking the Earth, and the each of them – abominations all – naked save for their silly blades, harmless to you, who've been made bloodless. You'll make them to dust, and your will shall be the dust's will, swilling out over the valleys and firths and high heaths until she subjugates herself before you, as in days past, before the stars slept. You'll hold out a cup for her to drink, and the ocean will rush ashore to drown the dust and cleanse the land of their defilement. So that at last you'll rule this hollow empty world with her alone at your feet, an eager slave to your will."

It was then I noticed an odd thing. His grin was still, his lips unmoving, as he stood speaking, staring straight through me. Yet his words roared in my head like a bull seal, and I grew faint from the boom of it.

"They speak of love, vain lappings of passions on the shore. What do they know of tunnels and peat deeps, of heather stained purple with blood, of the before and the after? Love is a weakness predicated on possession. To possess another is weakness. But to bring another into yourself, to create a thing in your own image: That's an expression of the universal will. It's the work of a god."

He closed his eyes, and I blinked. It was only a very brief blink, as long as it takes a thought to pass. Yet when I opened my eyes, he no longer stood before me but was busy washing up in the kitchen. The speed with which he must have moved there was astounding, scarcely credible.

I looked at the bed, where the contents of the box were spread. Something possessed me, I know not what, and I set about rearranging the items so that instead of lying in a row, they formed a circle, with the pencil in the centre. Why I would do such a thing, I cannot think, for circles are not particularly interesting, and circles with pencils in the centre are hardly more so. Seeing how the pencil lay there, splitting the circle in two, I removed it, then jabbed it point down, into the blanket directly in the middle of the circle. I did so with sufficient force that it remained upright, impaled in the blanket and the top layer of the mattress beneath.

The young man came in from the kitchen with a mug of tea. He saw how the items lay and glanced in my direction. Sitting at the writing table, he took up a pen and turned to a blank page in his book of fieldnotes. There he drew a large circle and within it a flower of seven petals, the tips of which touched the line of the circle. In the centre of the flower, he sketched out a figure, the form of a strange little man, sitting

I Have Not Answered

with crossed legs, tufts of hair sprouting from his skull. In the figure's hands, he drew a harp and a sort of cup.

His task complete, he shut the notebook and sat there in great stillness, still as the boulders at Eshaness.

Or as Foula out in the sea.

In my mind's eye, the great flats opened up before me, grass and rocks and emptiness and ocean as far as you can see. Dore Holm hulked up from the water, its arch of stone evidencing something I had forgotten, the passage of a great ancient thing or I know not what. Stone is a thing that is very old. It must have existed even before the time of those who came before, else how should they sleep within it?

The Northmen said the whole Earth was the corpse of an enormous dead thing. This, of course, is patently untrue, for else, where was the dead thing standing when it died? But then, the Northmen did not have telescopes and such at the time. Yet it would explain so much. And the Northmen said that the trows and crawling things and all that were but maggots burrowing in the flesh of this rotting world.

There was a knock at the door. It caught the young man and me by surprise, and we took a moment to rouse from our respective trances. The door opened, and May stepped in. She smiled at the young man. He forced a smile back, his eyes darting involuntarily toward the bed. May's eyes followed, but as she turned, her smile vanished. The brain does not immediately register the pictures that play upon the eye. Understanding takes a moment to form.

The young man leapt up. "May."

"Innes." Her face slackened as the items arranged on the bed took on significance.

Although he had his hand on her arm, she did not move, so he stepped between her and the bed, trying to block her gaze. But he was so thin, I do not think it achieved much. He tried drawing her back out the door, yet she proved immobile, looking over his shoulder at the bed.

"My things..."

"I found them. I found them in the hill."

It cut me deeply, this lie of his. It was not a half lie or even an evasion. The lie was full, unredeemable in its humanity.

"I found them in the hill when I was out walking. In a bag with a tuft of wool and some driftwood."

She looked at him in disbelief.

"I don't know. Someone must have taken them. I was going to go over to see you about it later today."

He added, "It's actually quite frightening, isn't it? To think..."

She stepped back, but not too far since he was still holding her arm. "Where?"

"I told you. In the hill." He looked down at the floor. "I..."

She removed his hand from her arm.

"I... I can't explain it."

"Innes."

"I don't know how they got here. I'd come into the room, and there'd be something on the bed. Or maybe something in the bathroom or in front of me when I was meditating.

I Have Not Answered

But I didn't know what to do with them, so I put them in a box and kept them under the bed. But I've nothing to do with it. You see? I've done nothing."

She closed her eyes, her lips mouthing words before she spoke. "How did you get them? Have you been in my room?"

He looked at the floor. "I've never been in your room. I just said. I found them." When he looked up, his eyes shone with a cold strength, as though reflecting the soullessness of another. "And why not? Why shouldn't I take what I desire?"

May shook her head. "You're sick. I can't help you."

"You don't understand." There was anger in his voice.

"Stay away from me."

"I love you."

"It's as I told you before: It's not your choice to make." She turned her back on him and stepped into the doorway.

How little she understood. She was unworthy of his mastery. "May..."

She was like other animals. I had known it all along. Now he hated her, surely, she who had twisted him into lies, who had, for an instant, made him human. Eternity is not for her sort, for one who is born, procreates, and makes a nest for maggots. There would be another in whom his desire could be fulfilled. Her death would be a relief to the world.

His face was dark and his eyes gaping wide and black, his eyes roaring like those of a bull seal. In this moment, I think, he awakened and saw everything—his whole truth stretched out like the strings of a harp, leading behind and before.

He lunged at her, slamming her against the doorframe. With preternatural quickness, he had a hand around her throat. Pushing down upon her, he forced her to her knees there in the doorway, and her eyes grew wide as his.

"By this sacrifice might the land be awakened to the law."

A whale that throws itself onto the beach can suffocate under its own weight.

She squirmed against him, but he was on top and had a strange power that made her struggles as insignificant as the crash of a worm upon a stone. His breath came out hot in the cold air, steaming into the afternoon dusk. Her breath did not come out at all.

My whole body tingled, fingertips set to explode.

She stilled herself and gazed up at him.

It was an expectant peace, the fulfilment of something old and quiet played out over her lips. She was prepared to accept the chalice he offered.

The young man saw this, and his grip loosened so that she drew in a quick little breath. He stooped, and lingered, his lips upon hers, she being too weak to resist his kiss, breathing shallowly through her nose when the space allowed.

Time spooled out around me, and if a truth existed, I did not know it. The generations tramped by on their eager pilgrimage to doom, a parade of babies transforming to a band of men and easing into a shambling line of blood-sloshed corpses that collapsed beyond the horizon. I could not see their end, but I knew it was there. And for a moment, I

I Have Not Answered

maybe even felt as though blood coursed through my veins too, that I was like them, stumbling through the folly of the endless cycle, beginning to rot from the moment of birth.

If I had possessed what they call tears, I might have wept.

The young man staggered back. He looked down at May, her back up against the doorframe and her legs spread out in front. It was a kind of sleep. Shaking, he knelt before her and placed two fingers upon her neck where, I suppose, he felt the journeying of her blood. He placed his ear near her lips, and her hot little breaths reached into him. She was yet living.

The young man swept the things off the bed, the items I had collected with such care scattering across the linoleum floor. He returned to May, lifted her, and placed her on the mattress, tucking her in the blanket and adjusting her head on the pillow.

He turned to where I stood and looked through me to the wall, hatred in his eyes. "This is how it ends."

Recently, I have found it pleasant to imagine I am sometimes visible to him, despite the gap between our essential natures, to imagine that he glances at me from time to time.

It is an idle fancy, but even for one such as I, there can be pleasure in imagining.

The young man left the cottage and walked down the slope along the coast. The sun lay low in the west, so that when he came out of the shadow of Murnin Kame, Foula crouched in its halo, dark and bitter in the sea.

He kept walking, on past the beach where lay the skittered bones of the seal, and on and on into the twilight. By the time he reached Netherdale, the clear night was around us.

But he continued on around Coppa Wick and above Sel Ayre until Deepdale lay before him, its hidden reaches beyond even the influence of the full moon, which lit the raised landscape a cold corpse white. He did not pause but descended into Deepdale, and I feared for him, for the time was not propitious, and on a night like this I could not follow.

Yet far from approaching, claws outstretched, the things in Deepdale all fled before him, as mist before the sun. They scattered out in panic, some even attempting to cross the sluggish burn, where they splashed and perished, shrieks echoing their damnation, bleeding out into the waters.

He threaded his way up Ramna Vord until at last he stood atop the ridge. He looked out to Foula, which glowed a pitiless silver in the moonlight. The island seemed so dead, you could have sworn it once had lived.

Again he entered Deepdale, and again the things there were anguished for it. Then he was back beside me above Sel Ayre. The wind had picked up in the interim, and it occurred to me that he must be cold without his jacket. But his movements were steady and measured as he began the return trip to the cottage.

In the morning, I thought, the crisis would be past. By then, he would have either killed May finally or explained things to her satisfaction. He can be very convincing.

I Have Not Answered

When he got to the beach near the cottage, however, he did not continue home but instead clambered onto the shingle. He passed the remnants of the seal and went into the shallow surf, the last gasps of the waves lapping up to his ankles.

Foula, level with us, beckoned, and a node in the back of my head throbbed with the beating of waves upon the Kame.

I wanted to call out to him, tell him to stop, but his name eluded me. How long had I spent in his company without having learned his name? If I called, surely he would answer.

There came a vision into my eyes, and I saw a girl holding a harp, her hair black as the full moon upon a calm sea. With all my will, I wished for her to smile, but her eyes were full of sorrow, and if they yet possessed a soul, I knew deep within that this would soon depart.

It was all a misunderstanding.

Foula grew on the horizon until it blocked out all else, and only Foula remained. Its silver slopes spoke softly, gently, stifling the stars with their monotonous music. But it was not music, no. It preceded the age of music, and its song was a song of the eternal round that turns and turns and comes to nothing, the rim of a cup, endless beneath your fingertip.

There are so many paths and tunnels. Some, I believe, lead across the sea. But what would be the point of following them? They all lead the same place. There is a little man in a little room, and he looks just like you.

The young man mouthed a word, and though I could not hear it, I knew it was *May*. He mouthed it as though it were a name. But I cannot recall anyone named May. If it were a name, you might think he was calling. But if you thought that, you would be mistaken, for it seemed more like an answer.

And I thought of a girl with long black hair whose skin was pink with blood, unspilled, warm and coursing within. I felt sure I knew her, though the vision was strange. Could this be May? Or was her name something else?

The young man moved deeper into the surf, wading out until it was about his waist. I wished to follow, but the water was lifeless and chill. Even for one such as I, who has seen so much, who has spent lives upon lives training for this sight, there are places I cannot follow and deeds I cannot do.

The memory came upon me all at once in a sheet of flame. This was the place. I had been here before, stood on this very beach, seen a figure in the water. Oh, in an instant I saw them, and I knew them all, every one I had forgotten. There lay behind me a whole eternity of lives. The sea, the hills, Foula even. If you look at them from far away, they are all the same.

The water came up over the young man's stomach.

It was I who poured the poison. It was I who held the cup.

The young man took a last look at Foula, then looked up at the stars and mouthed the word *May*. He closed his eyes and sank beneath the waters.

In five thousand years, I will have forgotten him.

Foula's song hit me as mockery on the wind, the far-off music of a harp.

I did not mean for it to end this way.

Acknowledgments

THE FIRST DRAFT of this novel was written in 2011 when I was an unwilling exile in Copenhagen. Thanks are thus due to those people who quite materially made this novel possible through the hospitality and friendship they showed me: Keith Alexander Bergman, Stinne Grydehøj, Carsten Jensen, Michael Lindgreen, Sally Birkenfeldt Rendal, Esben Rossel, Søren Stobbe, Jane Lustrup Sørensen, and many others. Further thanks are due to those who assisted me in improving this novel through its numerous drafts: Pernille Vedel Esmann, Liz Jensen, Kerry Kaleba, Karin Moitzi, Christina Neumayer, J.V. Noriega, Martin Skovhus, and especially Ron Johnstone. Any mistakes remain, of course, my own. Final thanks go to the people of Shetland.

About Shetland

SHETLAND LIES FAR OUT in the North Atlantic. Except for Hermaneuk Inn and the area around Murnin Kame, all of the places and islands in the novel are real. Like Innes Pitmedden, you too can gaze at Foula from Dale of Walls, descend into Deepdale, look out over Eshaness, visit Shetland Museum & Archives, drink a coffee at Peerie Shop Cafe, and (with a bit of assistance and a lot of nerve) have awkward sex on the Sletts.

Shetland was originally settled by peoples from mainland Scotland, but the islands acquired a Scandinavian culture with the arrival of the Vikings around the year 790 CE. In 1469, Shetland was transferred from Norway to the Kingdom of Scotland, yet the islands still retain a unique culture and dialect.

Learn more about the world of the novel:
www.ihavenotanswered.com

Printed in Great Britain
by Amazon